Pass Me the Ball

(All's Fair in Love and Sports)

Julie L. Spencer

DEDICATION

Pass Me the Ball is dedicated to Abigail Gould, the only female high school football player I've ever personally had the privilege of meeting!

ACKNOWLEDGMENTS

Beth, Lisa, Shannon, Britney, Deb, Lara, thanks for being the best critique partners I could ever ask for!

Lisa Rector, once again, thank you for your fantastic editing skills! Your eye for detail amazes me!

Brenda Walter, thanks for the beautiful cover design!

Thank you Clayton Spencer, Dr. Jerry Bailey, Tracy Bryant, Matt Schwarck, Jennifer Price, Angie Cheney, Shannon Prout, Cameron Linford, Jared Peless for your football advice.

To my Chapter-A-Day readers, thanks for being the best superfans an author could ask for! Also, thanks for your contributions and suggestions to make this story great. You guys are the best.

CHAPTER ONE

<u>Skyler</u>

"Hey, Skyler, who's the new cheerleader?" With his elbow, Logan nudged me, which snapped my focus away from the center of the football field. The humidity hadn't set in yet, and the dew-covered grass clippings clung to my practice cleats as he and I trudged to where our team was gathering.

The cheerleaders clumped into little cliques in their usual practice area near the bleachers, taking advantage of their tardy coach. If there had been a new student, they would all be gathered around her. Plus, I would have known about it. As captain of the varsity football team and star quarterback, I considered myself in the know about these things. I shielded my eyes with my hand to get a better look.

My girlfriend, Amberlyn, waved casually from across the field, and the girl beside her turned to look at me. My breath caught. It couldn't be—

The girl standing beside Amberlyn was not a new cheerleader. She wasn't new at all. Yet she was almost unrecognizable.

Her long, flowing blonde hair caught the morning sunlight and glinted in waves as it rested on the shoulders of her ratty practice jersey that looked exactly like the one I was wearing. Except where my jersey pulled against my pectoral muscles, hers pulled against—woah, I wasn't going there. While the cheerleaders displayed their tanned calf and thigh muscles under little shorts, her white football pants, covered in grass stains from last season, hugged her hips and curves.

"That's Jonnie," I choked out, halting my march to the fifty-yard line.

"No flippin' way," Logan said. I swear his jaw dropped. How cliché. Mine was hanging open as well. I snapped my mouth shut and gulped.

Jonnie turned to give Amberlyn a quick hug, then pulled the scrunchie from her wrist, and gathered her long hair into a sloppy ponytail. She grabbed the duffle bag, shoulder pads, and helmet that rested by her feet and smiled as she jogged toward us.

"Hey, guys," Jonnie said. Her exuberance at seeing us shone on her face. Was she wearing makeup? To football practice? No, she just had a sprinkling of freckles across her sun-kissed cheeks. "Did ya have a good summer? I haven't seen you in months."

Neither of us answered her, and I'm pretty sure our jaws hung open again.

"Guys?" Jonnie's brow creased. "Are you okay?"

"I thought you were a new cheerleader," Logan stammered.

"Yeah, right." She pushed his shoulder and guffawed. "Could you imagine *me* as a cheerleader?"

"Uh huh," Logan and I both answered. I finally gathered my wits and shook myself out of my stupor.

"Where've you been all summer?" I asked. What I wanted to ask was who was this beautiful woman standing in front of me and where did the old Jonnie go? Where was the tomboy who'd played on our football team for years? Where was my best friend?

"I went over to stay with my dad for eight weeks," she said. From where we lived in Grand Haven, right on the shoreline of Lake Michigan, her dad's house was two hours away near Central Michigan University, where he was a biology professor. "Bummer that I didn't get to hang out at the beach, but the good news is, my dad totally threw me like a million passes, so I kept in practice." Her voice rose at the end in a sing-song way that gave me goosebumps.

"In practice? For what?" Logan scratched his head.

"Touchdowns, you dork. What's wrong with you today?" She shook her head at Logan and then turned to me. "You'll be happy to know that I've been running between three and ten miles every single day, other than that week when we had, like, three feet of rain. But I ran a couple of 5Ks too, so it made up the difference. I won't let you down, captain." She punched me on the arm playfully.

"Touchdowns…" My voice trailed off as she ran toward the center of the field, calling out to some of the other guys.

"Jayce! Oh my gosh, I haven't seen you in forever!" She ran right into his arms, and he lifted her up and swung her around.

"Chica! What's up? You look amazing." Jayce set her back on her feet, and then she hugged Conner.

"Hello, beautiful," Conner said. "When did you grow up?"

"You're so funny, Conner." Jonnie laughed and batted at his arm like a… like a girl. Like a flirtatious, teenage girl.

"Oh, crud," I grumbled as the whole team gathered around the girl who was *not* our new cheerleader. She was our best wide receiver. "We have a problem."

CHAPTER TWO

<u>Jonnie</u>

It was so fun to see all the guys. I could tell they were all excited to see me too. Other than Skyler. He seemed almost mad at me. I wasn't sure why. Maybe because we were all standing around talking rather than getting started.

We'd have to save the reunion celebrations for later in the day. Maybe some of the guys would want to get brunch with me at Shea's Diner after practice.

"Warm it up," Skyler's gruff voice demanded from just outside the circle. "Run the perimeter of the field twice."

"Ah, man, come on," Jayce complained. "It's the first practice. Do we have to go around twice?"

"Nope—" Skyler stepped right up to look Jayce in the eye. "We'll go three times instead."

"Thanks a lot, Jayce," Connor mumbled as he

took off to the edge of the field. The rest of the guys on our team followed Connor, some grumbling, some resigned expressions.

I hung back to run with Skyler after he set down his gear. We'd always run together. We needed to be in sync. Perfect harmony. I needed to know what he was thinking all the time so I could be in the right position at the right time to make the plays count.

I needed to know instinctively if I was to be the decoy or his target, but the opposing team couldn't suspect either way. To have a connection that strong required years of working together. We had that unique connection.

Skyler didn't start a conversation. I'd love to claim we ran in companionable silence, but that wasn't the case. Our run was uncomfortable. I wasn't going to be the one to break the silence. If he was having a bad day, I would just be there for him, running by his side.

I chanced a sidelong glance at Skyler's profile. His chestnut hair was shorter. He usually styled it with a little gel to hold back the bangs that naturally flopped to the side. This more natural length didn't need gel and was probably cooler for the muggy Michigan summers.

He'd grown over the past three months. He looked like a man. A kinda hot man. Okay, a really hot man. Amberlyn was lucky to have him for a boyfriend. I wondered if I'd ever have a boyfriend.

Guys didn't see me like that, like a potential girlfriend. I was one of *them*. They talked about things in front of me that they would never say to a girl they liked or even a girl they wanted to hook up with. Their cadence changed when girls were around, but not with me.

Today I was at a loss for words. Part of me wanted to ask how Skyler's summer vacation had been. I was curious if he and Amberlyn had driven to the Upper Peninsula to go to the Hessel Boat Show again this year. I also wanted to know what strategies he had planned for our first game, just three short weeks from now. I wanted to know if he'd chosen a college yet, if he'd heard any talk of scholarships.

But I didn't ask him any of it. I just ran beside him. He barely acknowledged me, almost as if purposely avoiding eye contact. I wondered if my presence was annoying him.

Only a few of us were winded from the quick warm-up. It was obvious who had kept in shape over the summer and who had sat around playing video games and eating junk food. Aiden in particular looked a little green and clammy. We needed him on the defensive line. He needed to get back in shape, and fast.

When we sat on the grass to stretch, Connor sat particularly close and asked me in a low voice, "What are you doing after practice?"

"I was thinking about going to Shea's Diner and having brunch," I answered. "You wanna come?"

"Heck yeah," Connor said.

"Can I come too?" Jayce asked.

"Definitely, I want all of you to come." The guys

within earshot were all smiles. I noticed Skyler pull his brows into a scowl. *What's his problem?* I looked away.

"That's enough stretching," Skyler said much sooner than he normally would. "I want lunges to the fifty-yard line, side shuffles to the end zone, then walking knee hugs all the way back here."

"Weird sequence," Connor mumbled, but hopped to his feet. He offered me his hand to help me off the grass like a gentleman. "Milady."

"Why thank you, sir." I imitated my best Southern belle accent, slipped my hand into his, and let him pull me practically into his arms. I pushed him away playfully and brushed grass off my backside.

"I said *lunges*," Skyler called. Several of the guys around me seemed to wake up from a stupor.

I led the way, trying once again to be a good example. I almost felt like a mamma duck with all her little ducklings falling in behind. When we switched to side-shuffles at the fifty-yard line, I found them surprisingly easier than in years past. It was almost as if my center of gravity was more balanced now that I'd become a woman. I felt like a dancer and seemed to glide the rest of the way down the field. Walking knee hugs on the way back stretched my glutes perfectly. I was ready to start drills.

Skyler and Logan were the last two to complete the warm-ups and seemed to be in deep conversation when they came to a halt. They stood side by side as Skyler called, "Bring it in. Let's talk."

We formed a semicircle around them and waited

for direction. Connor and Jayce flanked me on either side, and I sensed a pattern. I had a feeling the three of us were going to be best friends this season. Skyler seemed to cock his head to the side while staring at the three of us. I cocked my head right back and raised my eyebrows. His expression shifted, as if remembering the task at hand, and he put his arm around Logan's shoulders.

"We have in our midst one of the best running backs in the district," Skyler said. Logan's mouth gaped as if this was news to him. He was good, yes. But the best? "Because of this, I intend to rely heavily on our running game this season."

My stomach dropped. There were two main plays in football: running plays and passing plays. The only plays that involved the wide receiver were passing.

He was rendering me irrelevant. What the heck?

I lowered my gaze and fought the emotions threatening to surface. My rule since elementary school had been to never cry on the football field. No matter how many times I got tackled, or how hard it hurt to hit the turf, I would not let them see me as anything less than their equal. I could handle anything physical they threw at me.

But getting snubbed by my quarterback? That hurt on a deeper level. I barely heard his remaining instructions and missed the opening play call.

The next thing I knew I was flat on my back, and Connor was leaning over me, with his hand outstretched. "Are you okay, Jonnie?"

I used his arm as leverage to hoist myself off the

ground, dusting off my backside. I was reminded of my earlier internal dialogue about not hurting when I got tackled. I take it back. That hurt. I looked up to Skyler scowling.

"Pick up the slack, Gillis. Get back in position." Skyler turned away and called out, "Same play."

Oh crap. What a way to start our first practice of the season. I was in trouble.

CHAPTER THREE

<u>Skyler</u>

"What the heck happened out there?" I shoved my helmet into my locker. "Babying her? Asking her to get together after practice? Ogling her like she's a… like she's a…"

"A girl?" Connor asked, eyebrows raised.

"Yes!" I threw my hands up in exasperation. Having a girl on the football team used to be no big deal. Back when she was a tomboy.

"I got news for you, captain." Connor stepped much too close to me, getting right in my face. "She *is* a girl."

"No, she's not," I stammered. "She's, she's Jonnie. We've played with her since preschool."

"You're right, she's not a *girl*," Jayce said. "She's a *woman*."

"Playing with her in preschool was never this

much fun," Aiden said with feigned innocence.

"You guys need to wash the drool off your faces," I said.

"I was just heading for the shower." Connor pulled his sweaty jersey over his head.

"I think I need a *cold* shower," Jayce said, reaching toward Connor for a fist bump.

"Relax, Skyler," Aiden said, patting me on the shoulder. "Let's get cleaned up so we can head over to the diner. I'm starved, and Jonnie said she wanted to sit with me." Aiden lumbered toward the shower room.

"Another challenge we need to address," I grumbled softly enough that Aiden didn't hear. He had gained an unhealthy amount of weight over the summer. I would need to work with him one-on-one and see if I could help him regain some focus.

"What're we gonna do about those guys?" Logan asked, coming up beside me in solidarity.

"Got any suggestions?" I spoke out of the side of my mouth.

"I'm leaning toward the cold shower on this one."

"You're as bad as the rest of them." I furrowed my brow and folded my arms across my chest.

"You are too," Logan said, bumping his shoulder against mine. "Admit it."

"I have a girlfriend." I gulped. Was I trying to convince him? Or myself?

Logan didn't respond. Just stood beside me while I squirmed, then chuckled, and walked toward the shower. "Maybe you should invite your girlfriend to come to brunch with us."

"Shut up, Logan," I called after him. He just laughed and kept walking.

CHAPTER FOUR

Jonnie

"Seriously, we'll go running together and stuff, okay?" I rested my hand on Aiden's arm. He sighed and smiled at me. "Afterward I'll beat you at Fortnite."

"Hey, I want to be your teammate," Connor said from across the table, his mouth half full of pancakes. His fork hesitated before plowing through the next stack on his plate.

"Not until you learn some table manners." I lifted my chin in mock superiority. "I'll have you guys acting like gentlemen by the end of the season."

"I don't need gentlemen," Skyler grumbled. "I need a strong defensive line."

"Which is why Aiden and I are going jogging this evening before we play video games." I draped my arm around Aiden's shoulders.

"Whatever." Skyler shoveled in another bite of scrambled eggs and slumped his shoulders.

"I have to do *something* to help out this team," I said, pulling my arm off Aiden's shoulders. "Since apparently we no longer need a wide receiver."

"What?" Jayce whipped his head around. "Yes, we do."

"You're not quitting, are you?" Connor asked.

"I wasn't planning to, but Skyler said he wanted to focus heavily on our running game."

All eyes turned on Skyler, proverbial daggers flying across the table. He shrugged and spoke around a mouthful of food, "I didn't say we'd stop needing our wide receivers."

"That was the way I interpreted your little speech," I said, crossing my arms and resting back against my chair. All conversation had stopped as we waited to see how Skyler would respond. He looked around at the accusing eyes of our teammates and gulped down the bite of food he had in his mouth.

"Fine, we'll up our passing game," Skyler said, setting aside his fork. "But you guys need to get focused. If you want to set up brunch dates with each other, do it after practice. Quit flirting with our best wide receiver like she's a girl."

"But she *is* a girl," Connor said.

"And I *really* like flirting with her," Jayce added, draping his arm across my shoulders.

"And I really like catching footballs," I said with a smirk.

"Fine," Skyler said.

"Fine." I nodded my head definitively, sure I'd won the argument.

"I expect you on the field in two hours ready to run plays." Skyler pushed back his chair, stood, and reached into his back pocket for his wallet. He tossed a $10 bill in front of his half-eaten breakfast and stormed from the room.

CHAPTER FIVE

<u>Skyler</u>

I needed a nap.

But I told Jonnie two hours and thought it best to be here early. Not early enough, apparently. Jonnie was sitting cross-legged in the middle of the field, with her wrists resting on her knees, as if she was... meditating?

"Dude, what are you doing?" I called to her when I was ten feet away, and she still hadn't noticed me approaching. Her eyes were hooded, but open, sort of. She shook out of her stupor and smiled when she noticed me. Crap, why'd she have such a beautiful smile?

"You're here," she said. She didn't move.

"Stating the obvious?" I sat directly in front of her and crossed my legs, mirroring her. I twirled a football in my right hand as if it were a drumstick.

"Why are you mad at me?" She still didn't move.

"What's this yoga thing you got going on?" I asked.

"You didn't answer my question."

"You didn't answer mine."

"I asked you first." She lifted her chin. She had me.

"I'm not mad at you." Did my voice just drop an octave? How embarrassing. "You just seem different this year, and it startled me."

"I was meditating," she said.

Oh yeah, I'd asked. I continued my line of thinking. "You've grown up. You look like a woman."

"And *you* look like a man," she said and then smirked. "You're kinda hot. I'm a little jealous of Amberlyn."

"You have nothing to be jealous about." I absentmindedly picked grass out of the field. Wait—what did I just say? "I mean… um… Amberlyn has no reason to be jealous. I mean—weren't we gonna run some plays?"

I stood quickly and almost reached down to help her up, but instead, I took two steps back and held up my football again.

"On your feet, Gillis. Let's go."

She chuckled but rose from the field, too gracefully I might add, and brushed the grass off her rear end. She really needed to stop doing that. I turned and walked toward the forty-yard line.

"Let's work on your short pass first, and then we'll

go long," I instructed. "Set it up for a hook."

She followed me to the line of scrimmage, lined up at the split end position, and nodded. "Ready, captain."

CHAPTER SIX

<u>Jonnie</u>

"Now, because Jonnie's faster than... well... pretty much everyone in the league, she'll be able to get out ahead of the defense, but that doesn't mean we don't have to stop them from getting to her." Skyler looked up from his handheld white board where he'd been drawing plays.

The cross-country team had been trying to recruit me since middle school but I was committed to football. During track season, I held several records in the 800, open and relay, and the two-mile. But football was my passion and I'd been playing on the guys' teams since sixth grade flag football.

"They won't get past us; I can promise you that," Jayce said, winking at me.

"You need to be blocking for Logan when he's the ball carrier," Skyler said. As the tight end, Jayce was frequently called on to block, especially during running plays. If he wasn't paying attention, Logan could be pummeled by the defense.

"Well, when Logan's *not* rushing," Jayce said through gritted teeth, "I'll block for Jonnie. And who made you the offensive coach?"

"You also need to get open if I can't get the ball to her for whatever reason." While they waited for Coach Bryant to get off the phone, Skyler ignored Jayce questioning his limited authority and looked around to meet everyone's eyes. "And even though you're all in charge of blocking for our receivers, don't forget about me."

"I've got your blind side, captain." Connor nodded definitively. "No one's getting past me." Connor offered Skyler a fist bump, and he returned it with gratitude. Connor was the best offensive tackle I'd ever seen. Skyler rarely got hurt on the field.

"Doug, you're our second-best wide receiver, so you'll often be the intended target to throw off the defense." Skyler met Doug's gaze.

"Gee, thanks." Doug rolled his eyes.

"I'm just being real," Skyler said. "You know darn well Jonnie's faster and more consistent. But the defense is going to be focusing on her, so you need to be ready."

"I'll be ready," Doug grumbled.

"I'm serious. You and I are gonna be stayin' after practice if you don't catch everything I send your way."

"I won't let you down, man." Doug gulped and

averted his eyes.

"The three of us will work together until we know what each other are thinking," I added. Skyler was right. Without Doug fully committed, our season would not go well.

Doug reached over, and we bumped fists. "I won't let you down either, girlfriend."

"Woah, woah, woah," Connor interjected. "She is *not* your girlfriend."

"She's not *anyone's* girlfriend," Skyler warned. "We've talked about this, guys."

There were grumbles around the huddle as the boys accepted the chastisement.

Skyler was right. I was definitely not anyone's girlfriend. They usually didn't even treat me like a girl. At least, last year they didn't.

"We may not have that problem." Coach Bryant approached the team with pursed lips. "I just got off the phone with the president of the league board. They insist Jonnie not play this season."

CHAPTER SEVEN

<u>Skyler</u>

"They can't do that," I said, standing and letting my white board out fall into the grass.

"They know that." Coach Bryant shook his head. "They're just being jerks. They're probably hoping *we* don't know that, and they can bully us into keeping her on the bench."

"Why don't they want me to play?" Jonnie stood beside me, her arm brushing against mine. I was tempted to take her hand in solidarity but fought the inclination.

"They claim you might get hurt, and they don't want to be responsible for that," coach explained. "They say the officials don't want to deal with the risks, and the other teams will be hesitant to tackle you because you're a girl, which would give you an unfair advantage."

"In other words, the other teams are scared we're going to beat them." Jayce sauntered up beside Jonnie and draped his arm over her shoulders. "Because we have the best wide receiver in the league."

"In the state, probably," Logan said.

"Yeah, well, my daddy's the best attorney in the state," Connor piped in. "And I'm not afraid to call on him."

"I'm sure that won't be necessary, gentlemen." Coach stopped and smiled and then nodded to Jonnie regally. "And lady."

She lifted her chin and grinned. "I don't get called a lady very often."

"Well, gee, I think you should." I had an idea and turned to Jonnie with a conspiratorial grin. "I think every Friday night you should be the first player off the bus and should be dressed up, hair and makeup done, the works. Show them what a lady looks like, and then show them what a lady can do on the field."

"I like your idea." Jonnie's grin was wide and so beautiful it hurt to look at it. "I'm going to need Amberlyn's help to make it happen, but I think we can handle it."

"This is going to be our best season ever," Jayce said. "I can't wait for our first game."

CHAPTER EIGHT

<u>Jonnie</u>

"Hey, guys!" Amberlyn called as she ran to the center of the field. "We're planning an end of summer beach party this Saturday, and you're all invited."

She rested her hand on Skyler's arm and my stomach tensed. Why should I be jealous? She was his girlfriend. Maybe because her cheerleading shorts displayed beautifully tanned legs and my grubby practice pants hid bruised knees and stubble that I hadn't shaved since I'd gone to the beach weeks ago, with my dad and stepmom, and made sandcastles, with my little half-brother and -sister.

The football players purposefully kept their gazes at eye-level to avoid Skyler's wrath should he ever catch them ogling his girlfriend. I was allowed to be jealous. She was my best friend after all. But they weren't allowed to covet.

"You're going to have to take me shopping for a new swimsuit," I told Amberlyn. "I left my old one at my dad's."

"There should be plenty on sale," Amberlyn said. "It's the end of the season, after all. We could go shopping after practice."

"After I go home and shower off this mud and scrape the stubble from my legs."

"Do you need any help picking out a swimsuit?" Jayce rested his arm around my shoulders. "I could sit outside the dressing room, and you can come out and model them for me."

"Uh, no." I extricated myself from under his arm. "I would be totally embarrassed for anyone to see me in a swimsuit."

"What are you going to do at the beach?" Skyler asked. He and the rest of the team had dropped jaws, and Amberlyn cocked her head to the side.

"Well, um, I'll probably keep my T-shirt on?"

"Then why shop for a suit at all?" Skyler asked. He creased his eyebrows.

"It's a girl thing," Amberlyn said, draping her arm through mine. "Maybe if you all stop drooling over her like she's a supermodel, she'd relax, and we can get her out of that T-shirt."

"Okay, you talking about getting her out of her T-shirt is not helping," Connor said. "Forget football practice. We're all going to need cold showers."

"See what I've had to put up with all these years, Amberlyn? They joke around like I'm one of the guys."

"I'm pretty sure they're not joking anymore," she stage-whispered and then turned to me with a smile. "Because you've sort of got the body of a super model now."

"Oh please." I snorted.

"You could always come join the cheerleading squad."

"No, we'll stop!" Jayce stepped closer to me again and wrapped both arms around me in a backward hug. I didn't fight him off this time but, for some reason, glanced at Skyler to catch his reaction. Skyler wasn't looking at me. He was looking at Amberlyn.

"Them are fightin' words, woman," Skyler said to Amberlyn. "You're not stealing our best wide receiver. No offense, Doug." He barely glanced to my fellow receiver.

"None taken," Doug answered. "Trust me, I don't want to lose her either. Too much pressure on me."

"There's no way I'm abandoning my team," I said. "Now, go be a cheerleader for a couple hours, and I'll kick these guys' butts for a while. Then you and I can go shopping for the perfect suit... for me to hide under my T-shirt."

"Sounds like a plan." She stepped closer to Skyler and leaned in for kiss. I looked away. "Have fun you guys."

CHAPTER NINE

<u>Skyler</u>

"Pickup game?" I held a football in my right hand, pretending I wasn't looking at any one person. I had dark shades on so my friends lying on beach towels couldn't necessarily tell in what general direction my gaze was aimed.

"In the water? Or on the sand?" Jonnie asked, without sitting up or removing her sunglasses. From where I stood, she didn't look as if she'd moved, but I'd recognize that voice anywhere. She lifted her head off her beach towel and shaded her eyes to look up at me.

"Both?" A grin spread on my face that mirrored hers. "Nothing above the knee, or the dry sand." That got other kids' attention, even some of the non-football players.

We'd met at Buchanan beach, away from the

tourist trap of the Grand Haven State Park, or one of the Ottawa County parks. This place was just for the local teens. One last gathering before school started the following week.

Derek, my backup quarterback, met me at my shoulder. "Schoolyard pick, captain?"

"Sure, you want to pick first?" I offered. "Ya know, to make it fair?"

"Jonnie," Derek said without hesitation.

"Ah, come on, man."

"You said you wanted to make it fair."

"Should I be flattered that y'all are fightin' over me?" Jonnie asked, already off her towel and brushing the sand off.

I was momentarily distracted at how cute she looked in the little shorts and tank swimsuit she and Amberlyn had chosen. They called it a compromise. I called it adorable. All the other girls, including my own girlfriend, seemed to compete for who could wear the least amount of clothing and still pretend they were properly covered. They left little to the imagination. I preferred the more modest approach.

Jonnie reached down for Doug's hand to hoist him up from the towel beside her. "Guess you're my opponent today?"

"You're on, Gillis," Doug said, taking his place by my side.

"I get to choose next since that decision was made for me," I said. "I want Logan." He joined my side.

"Connor," Derek said.

"Jayce," I fired back.

"Aiden." Derek gave Aiden a high five.

"Amberlyn," I called out, wondering if my girlfriend would play football with me if I asked her to be on my team.

"Are you crazy, baby?" Amberlyn sat up halfway and propped herself on her elbows. "I just had my nails done." She held up one hand and waved them at me.

Several other girls, including Jonnie, leaned in to see the pretty jewels Amberlyn had paid big money to have inlaid in her unnaturally long acrylics.

"It was worth a shot." I shrugged. "Can't say I didn't ask."

"I wish I could get my nails done," Jonnie said, standing straight again and examining her hands.

"Ah, Jonnie," Connor said, reaching for her hands. "Your hands are perfect just the way they are. You don't need all that sparkly stuff."

Was he flirting? Or making fun of her? I couldn't tell.

A different girl, someone not in our usual circle of friends, asked, "Why can't you get your nails done?"

"They would get in the way of her catching the football." With confused shock, Connor looked down at the girl. "They would break during the first game."

"Why would anyone want to catch a football?" the girl asked.

I glanced down at the ball in my hands, wondering if she were making a generalization or just referencing girls. I could think of about fifteen people within my arm's reach who would have an argument with that, including the one with the long, blonde braid and the adorably modest swimsuit.

Jonnie raised her chin and stepped back within our little cluster of guys and looked down at the girl. "I am the best wide receiver on the Buccaneers' football team. No offense, Doug." Without glancing at Doug, she lifted her hand for a fist bump.

"None taken, babe."

"Skyler"—Jonnie turned to me—"Go long."

Without waiting for my answer, she took off down the beach at a speed the track stars were envious of, and I hauled back my arm, waiting until just the right moment. I launched a perfect spiral while she was still running away, trusting she would instinctively know when to stop. She did. When she turned, she adjusted her direction and hooked to the left, reached for the ball, and practically caught it one-handed. *Wow.*

"What a woman," Jayce said.

I couldn't disagree. I also couldn't take my eyes off her as she jogged easily back and stood directly in front of the girl who had asked the stupid question.

"You asked why anyone would want to catch a football?" Jonnie said. "I'll throw the question right back at ya. Why *wouldn't* I want to catch a football?"

"I suppose if I could catch that well, I'd avoid manicures too." The girl bit her lip and looked around at the group, obviously trying to save face.

"Thank you." Jonnie nodded, then backed away from the girl and trudged through the sand over to me, holding out the football. "Your ball, captain."

"Oh, I think you earned that, Gillis." Did my voice soften? How embarrassing. I tried to pull my gaze away from hers, very aware we were surrounded by our peers, none of whom realized I couldn't breathe, and my heart was racing. I really tried. I gulped. Thankfully she looked away first.

Jonnie stepped over to Derek and handed him the ball. "I guess we get to be on offense first."

"Awesome." Derek called out, "Set it up."

A few other guys, and even a couple girls, joined us, and we gave each of our teams some instructions and pep talks and then got started.

Playing defense was unnatural, but with this few people, the only option was to play both sides of the line of scrimmage. I positioned myself on the opposite end of the lineup from Jonnie, needing a break from gazing at her before I got into trouble.

Derek started off with a running play and soon one of our second-string running backs, a kid named Steve, had the ball. Logan—not one to allow his competition to best him—took off after Steve and tackled him to the sand.

They laughed and brushed themselves off and then ran back toward the rest of us. We drew a new line in the sand, since technically the distance traveled was enough to be a first down. Their team was now closer to their predetermined pylon acting as the end zone.

When we lined up again, I didn't pay close enough attention and found myself directly in front of

Jonnie. I locked eyes with her, suspecting she was the intended target this play. Sure enough, she took off down the beach at full speed, and I kept up, preparing to take her down the minute that ball was in her hands.

She turned to see if the ball was at her shoulder, as it would have been if I'd thrown it. She had to adjust to Derek's inaccurate throw by running into the waves. In true Jonnie fashion, she found a way to capture that ball out of thin air.

With no hesitation, I tackled Jonnie in waist-deep waves, plunging into the water, with her in my arms. She came up sputtering, but with the ball still in her clutched hands. *Impressive.*

I helped her to her feet, and she held up the ball for her team to see. "Touchdown!"

I heard cheering behind me, but I couldn't take my eyes off her again. What the heck was wrong with me?

A wave pulled at us, and she grasped my arm with one hand to steady herself. I instinctively held her up, and before I realized what had happened, I'd pulled her close. That was the moment another wave rolled in and knocked us all the way into the water again.

I didn't hurry to help her this time. I enjoyed just a few more seconds with her in my arms, lying there as the waves rolled over us. Knowing I needed to pull myself out of this compromising position, I disentangled myself and struggled to stand. I offered her my hand, and she pulled herself up.

Our eyes met and held as we breathed hard from

the run and the fall, and—who was I kidding? From being in each other's arms.

I'd held Amberlyn in my arms hundreds of times in the past three years, even made out with her a few times. But nothing with Amberlyn felt like this. Nothing in my life had ever felt like this.

"Hi," I whispered.

"Hi." She stared up at me and gulped.

"We'd better get the football back over to our teams…"

"Can't play without the football," she answered.

"That was a heck of a catch."

"That was more than a catch," Jonnie said, her eyes conveying a message neither of us could vocalize. "It was a touchdown."

"It was a heck of a touchdown."

"You and I are pretty good at getting touchdowns, aren't we?" she asked.

"Yeah," I agreed. "We are."

"We need to get the football back over to our teams…"

"Yeah, we do." Neither of us moved.

"Okay…"

"Okay."

Hanging on to each other's arms—for stability—we trudged out of the surf; then she pushed me playfully and ran ahead, holding the football high like a trophy, waving to her team.

I let out a long breath, watching her run ahead. "I'm in trouble."

CHAPTER TEN

<u>Jonnie</u>

"Wow, I look amazing." I turned every which way, marveling at the transformation in the full-length mirror in Amberlyn's bedroom. "You have worked magic."

"You've never looked more like a girl." Amberlyn clapped her hands in excitement. "I can't wait for everyone to see you."

I even felt like a girl, which was rare. Living next door to one another had its advantages, including getting ready for school together on the first day. Amberlyn had carefully rolled curls along the length of my silky blonde hair and had given me instructions on how to recreate the look on my own.

My makeup was more subdued. I didn't want too much effort to get ready for practice at the end of the day, and games would require even less prep time between getting off the bus and being on the field in my uniform. Just a little waterproof mascara and light lip gloss.

The real magic was in the hair and clothes. I planned to don a skirt almost as short as the cheerleaders on Friday nights to throw off the opposing team but, for the first day of school, felt it best to tone things down. I chose a black calf length pencil skirt with a pink tunic that showed off every curve. They paired well with my new little, white Vans shoes and classic Bobbie socks.

"Okay, enough primping," Amberlyn said, grabbing her backpack. "Skyler will be here to pick us up any minute."

"Hey, babe, you almost ready?" As if on cue, Skyler poked his head in the door and stopped short. His jaw dropped. "Dude, what the *heck* did you do?"

"Am I a miracle worker or what?" Amberlyn grasped Skyler's arm in excitement and bounced up and down like a little girl.

I twirled as if I were at the end of a runway and placed my hand on my hip like a supermodel. "Do you think I'll turn some heads today?"

"Uh…" Skyler just stared.

"Skyler, answer her." Amberlyn pouted. "Doesn't she look beautiful?"

"She's always been beautiful," Skyler whispered. Amberlyn's face fell, and Skyler woke up from his stupor. He turned and wrapped his arm around his crestfallen girlfriend. "Now she looks like a beautiful *girl*. Yes, you are a miracle worker."

Skyler leaned forward and pressed a quick kiss to Amberlyn's lips.

I had to look away. I walked over to Amberlyn's bed and lifted my backpack onto one shoulder, glancing once more in the mirror before heading out the door.

CHAPTER ELEVEN

<u>Skyler</u>

I'd almost messed up. I still wasn't sure how I was supposed to feel. But walking in that first day, I had the hottest cheerleader in the school on my right arm, and to my left the hottest girl on the football team.

Okay, the only girl on the football team, but likely the hottest topic of conversation. Most of the student body hadn't known of Jonnie's transformation over the summer and probably thought the same thing I'd thought when I'd first seen her—new cheerleader.

Jayce was quick to shove me out of the way when we walked up to where the team congregated in the foyer by the gym. "Look at you!" Jayce wrapped his arm around Jonnie's waist, effectively claiming her.

Jonnie bumped her hip against his and batted her

eyelashes, flirting playfully. Her expression changed, and she dismissed Jayce when she saw Aiden. "Oh my gosh, Aiden, you look amazing!"

She jumped toward Aiden's outstretched arms and allowed him to pull her into a hug. I had to admit Aiden's transformation had been almost as dramatic as Jonnie's. His hulking form had trimmed down thanks to Jonnie dragging him out jogging every evening.

Because I saw him every day in his jersey and pads, I hadn't realized how fit Aiden looked in slacks and a button-down shirt. He'd pulled out the nice clothes for the first day of school, that or he was trying to show off his new-and-improved body. A pang of jealousy pulled at my stomach for the second time in two minutes, and I turned away to wrap my arm more firmly around Amberlyn's waist. "You ready to get to first hour?"

By the time we turned to head down the hall, Jonnie was flanked by guys and led in the point position toward our first class. Standing several feet behind the pack, I had the chance to witness everyone in the crowd do a double take when they noticed the hot new girl with her pack of disciples.

Little did they know that hot new girl wasn't new, and she was about to shake up the world of high school football. I was excited to have a front row seat.

CHAPTER TWELVE

Skyler

"Do you have any friends on the cheerleading squad who need boyfriends?" I knew my question would catch Amberlyn off guard, but I needed her help with an idea. We'd been dating forever, and I knew I could trust her.

She had a few French fries clasped in her fingers halfway to her mouth, and her jaw dropped. "What?"

"The football players need girlfriends, so I want to hook them up." I picked up my cheeseburger and tried to catch the special sauce from dripping all over the wrapper as I took the first bite.

"I don't understand what you mean." Amberlyn finally shoved the fries into her mouth and reached for her Coke. The condensation from the cup left a ring on the cheap Formica table. A few kids ran by on their way to the playscape area, but I pulled my attention back to the matter at hand.

"The guys on the football team are fawning over

Jonnie." I grabbed a napkin to swab up the mess I was creating all down my hands.

"And…" She lifted her eyebrows.

"And it's a distraction." I thought it was so obvious.

"So, what do the cheerleaders have to do with this?" she asked more directly this time.

"If I could get these guys some girlfriends, they would stop fawning over her."

"What is it with you and her?" Suspicion laced Amberlyn's question, and she shoved aside her half-eaten chicken sandwich.

"What do you mean?" I took apart my burger under the pretense of scraping off the extra sauce, but I used the distraction as a way of averting my eyes from her accusing stare. "We've been best friends for years."

"I thought I was your best friend." Amberlyn pouted and folded her arms, leaning back in the booth.

"You're my girlfriend. There's a difference."

"But if your best friend is a girl, doesn't that make *her* your girlfriend?"

"I thought we were talking about getting girlfriends for the football players." I changed tactics. "Think about it. Jonnie can only go with *one* of them to the homecoming dance, so we need dates for everyone else. We can go as a big group and hopefully some of them will pair off. Have you bought a dress yet?" Good diversion. Shopping. Girls loved shopping. And the homecoming dress was an important thing to shop for. I took a huge bite of my hamburger to shut myself up.

"No, a couple of us from the cheerleading squad are going shopping on Saturday. Maybe I can invite Jonnie to go with us. Do you know who's taking her to the dance?"

I choked a little and had to take a sip of pop. The thought of Jonnie dancing with someone else made my stomach flip. "No."

"It's gonna be a bloodbath once they figure out she doesn't have a date yet," Amberlyn said with a giggle. "They'll be falling all over themselves to be the first to ask her."

"All the more reason to get a group together." I jumped on this tactic. "We'll make sure the guys in the group all know that they have to keep the girls in the group dancing. Like they're all each other's dates, ya know?"

"Uh… sure. Sorta. I guess I'll have to think about this." Amberlyn prattled on about who already had boyfriends and who didn't, and who she wouldn't recommend that any of my friends go out with because they were gossiping brats, and which of her friends would look best in pink dresses rather than red, but how autumn colors might be a better choice for this time of year. I tried to keep up and reminded myself this was my idea.

It was a good idea.

I leaned my elbow on the table and listened more intently. Yeah, this could work.

CHAPTER THIRTEEN

<u>Jonnie</u>

Skyler had been right that me showing up at the game looking like a lady would have the desired effect on the opposing team. I subtly flipped my long hair over my shoulder, relishing the weight of the curls and wondering why I didn't curl my hair years ago.

Our first game was also our home opener, and I turned heads all the way to the locker rooms. I had to part ways with the guys and head into the ladies' room where the entire cheerleading squad was readying themselves to take the field, with the welcome banner.

The girls on the cheerleading squad squealed when I walked in and gathered around to give me hugs. "You go girl!" "Knock 'em dead, tiger!" "You look amazing!"

"Thanks, guys," I said. "I need to go get changed into my uniform."

"Are you going to remove your eye makeup?" Amberlyn asked. "Do you need any help?"

"No, the waterproof mascara has withstood heat and sweat all week at practice. I think I'm good."

I ducked into the largest stall in the restroom, where I'd hung my jersey and pads earlier that day. Usually I pulled all my hair back and tucked a braid inside my helmet, but not anymore. I decided to carry my helmet for now and purposely draped my curls in a cascade across my shoulders.

With a determined grin, I started toward the door of the locker room. "Wish me luck, ladies."

Our team was waiting outside, and we ran together toward the center of the field for practice. Just prior to starting practice, I made a point to twist my hair up into a scrunchy and rest my helmet gracefully on top.

I lunged and stretched and ran ladders alongside the guys and then ran long into the end zone and caught an easy practice pass that looked more impressive than it actually was.

Then we ran back to await the welcome banner. Coach Bryant offered a traditional pep talk just outside the locker rooms since it would have been inappropriate for me to sit with the guys inside.

When the cheerleaders had their banner set, I took my position next to Skyler, just off his flank, making it very clear to onlookers who the captain was and who his right-hand receiver was. We broke the banner at full speed, and I relished the hometown excitement of the first game of my senior year.

CHAPTER FOURTEEN

<u>Skyler</u>

I'd been right. The other team was flustered to the point of an easy victory. Logan had rushed for 150 yards and ran in one touchdown. Doug had caught every pass, as had Jayce. Connor protected me as if his life depended on it, and Aiden had recovered a fumble to run in a fifty-five-yard pick six.

But Jonnie had been the real star of the show, as planned.

She dashed down the field faster than the other team could get their bearings and never risked a tackle once. Using her as a decoy over and over led the other team to grow confused and complacent, which allowed me to have an open receiver nearly every play.

The biggest frustration was after the game. Jonnie went into the girls' locker room, and we went into ours. I felt an almost physical pain of separation when the rest of the team—without her, my best friend—surrounded me.

Was Amberlyn correct? Was Jonnie more of a girlfriend than a best friend?

I'd been dating Amberlyn since our freshman year of high school when I'd served as the student council president and she'd been the vice-president. We'd done everything together for several weeks, and the homecoming dance had been approaching. I asked her to come with me on a whim, and we'd been together ever since.

Amberlyn had never questioned my relationship with Jonnie until now. Maybe that was because Jonnie hadn't looked like a girl until now. Or maybe because my face was too easy to read, and I could no longer hide my true feelings.

The cheerleaders had some sort of planned overnight together, so I wouldn't see Amberlyn after the game. I didn't see Jonnie either. I wondered if she'd gone with the other girls to hang out.

When I left the locker room, the lights of the stadium were still burning bright, and a few people mingled in the stands and near the fences. I carried my shoulder pads to my car and sat inside, listening to music and waiting for the lights to turn off. Years ago, I'd started a habit of heading back onto the field alone in the dark. Something about the empty stadium after a game gave me peace and closure for the night.

I waited ten minutes after the stadium went black,

hoping most people would have left. Most had. One had not. I knew exactly who was sitting cross legged at the center of the fifty-yard line. I hesitated a few seconds, watching her, sensing what would happen if I dared venture out to disturb her.

"What are you doing, Skyler?" I mumbled to myself as my feet carried me forward. "You have a girlfriend. You have a girlfriend. You have a girlfriend."

I expected her to maintain a trance as I approached, as she'd done the day of our first practice. She didn't. As if sensing my presence, Jonnie turned her head and watched me.

"Hey," she called softly when I was ten feet away.

"Whatchu doin' out here?" My voice cracked. I lowered myself to the grass beside her, leaned back on my hands, and gazed up at the stars.

"Same thing you're doing," Jonnie said.

"I highly doubt that," I mumbled. What I was doing was thinking inappropriate thoughts about the woman who used to be a girl sitting beside me in the moonlight. The same girl who used to be a tomboy. The tomboy who used to toss a football back and forth and play video games and go jogging. I doubted she was thinking about the cheerleader who was counting on me to be faithful.

"Great first game, huh?" Jonnie's voice was subdued. This wasn't a high-five kind of question. There was underlying meaning. Deeper meaning. What was she really asking? What was my answer? I answered her question with a question of my own.

"Do you remember the day we met?" I asked.

"The first day of preschool?" she guessed.

"I thought you were a boy." I bit my lip sheepishly.

"It was the hair, wasn't it?" Jonnie chuckled. "I cut it myself with the kitchen scissors. My mom was so angry, but I was tired of her putting it up in braids with pink ribbons."

"By the time I figured out you were a girl, it was too late. You were already my best friend."

"You were the only one who could beat me in a foot race." She shrugged.

I took a deep breath and steeled myself for where I knew this conversation had to go. "I swear this has nothing to do with your looks. I'm not that shallow. But you're kinda *more* than my best friend now."

"I know." She picked grass from the field and lowered her gaze. The freshly cut field from earlier in the day was trampled and muddy but it smelled like football season.

"Something changed over the summer. I'm not a boy anymore, and quite frankly, you're not a girl anymore. The guy in me thinks you are smokin' hot, and it scares the heck out of me."

"The feeling is mutual," Jonnie whispered.

"I know. I can see it in your eyes, or I wouldn't have said anything."

"What are we gonna do?"

"I can't break up with Amberlyn right now," I said.

Jonnie turned away, and her shoulders hunched. I

panicked and tried to turn her back around. When that didn't work, I wrapped my arms around her and pulled her close.

"It's not that I don't want to," I said, a lump forming in my throat. "The timing would be horrible. People would think I was dumping her because you grew up over the summer and can catch every football I throw at you. Do you know how bad that would look?"

She didn't answer.

"Give me a couple of weeks to figure this out, okay? Go to the homecoming dance with one of your disciples and wear a pretty dress and make me jealous to the point of distraction."

She chuckled and wiped at her eyes, leaning back against me. The chill in the late summer night was obvious with her warmth in my arms.

"I haven't kissed Amberlyn in weeks," I whispered. "I just wanted you to know that."

"You kissed her on Tuesday," Jonnie said. "I saw you."

"That was a peck," I said. "You knew what I meant. I mean, *really* kissed her. And I don't plan to."

Jonnie laid her head on my shoulder, and I realized my lips were very close to her neck, just below her jaw. The temptation was overwhelming.

That was the moment the automatic sprinklers turned on.

We jumped up from the grass and ran toward the building where the locker rooms and concession stand were dark and locked. We laughed and shook the water from our arms and faces and hair.

Our eyes met, and our laughter halted. My breathing was heavy, either from running off the field, of the nervousness of what I knew I wanted to do.

I took a step forward, laced my hands into Jonnie's hair, and cradled her head while searching her eyes illuminated only by moonlight. I hesitated and pressed my forehead against hers, desperate to kiss her, knowing I shouldn't. For one incredible moment, I held her before choosing the impossible.

I released her gently and walked away.

CHAPTER FIFTEEN

<u>Jonnie</u>

Practice the following day should have been easy. We were coming off our first game and our first big win. But I had to look Skyler in the eye after he'd almost kissed me the night before.

And I had to pretend it never happened.

I had to pretend everything was normal. I had to let them all congratulate me and talk about their favorite plays and comment on that huge linebacker on the opposing team. I had to avoid looking at Skyler.

There was no shortage of distractions. All the guys wanted to sit next to me while we watched the recap in the coach's classroom. Jayce won the coveted spot on my left, and Connor managed to monopolize my right, but I was very aware of Skyler sitting behind me in the darkness.

He leaned forward after we watched a particularly good play, and his breath was close to my ear. "That was a heck of a catch, Gillis."

I fought the urge to lean back and let him hold me again. Before he sat back, he nudged his head against mine. It was something. I was certain no one else noticed, but it meant something to me. As if he was reaching out to offer just a tiny recognition that last night hadn't been a fluke. We may not be able to show each other affection in public, but he wanted me to know he was there.

My eyes closed involuntarily, and I inhaled the scent that was uniquely Skyler. We hadn't started actually practicing yet, so none of the guys were sweaty and gross. They all seemed to come to practice freshly showered and wearing cologne, as if they were still hoping I'd notice them.

I noticed them all right. I noticed them in the way I'd notice a mosquito buzzing around my ear while I was trying to sleep. I didn't want to encourage any of them, yet I still needed all of them in my corner. This football team was like a family to me.

Coach Bryant turned the lights back on, and we all sat up straighter. "At the behest of sounding overly congratulatory, and overconfident, I'll start by telling you how proud I am of you."

"Yeah, nice job, everybody." Skyler clapped his hands in a way that showed his leadership and didn't imply we should all join in.

"Nice job to you too, Skyler," coach said, pointing a football at him. "A team is only as good as the quarterback who can hit the targets."

"And thank you to the defense for stopping the other team." Skyler deflected the attention.

"Shoot, all Jonnie had to do was smile real pretty, and they all just sort of stepped aside," Jayce said.

"Very funny." I rolled my eyes but had to force to maintain a neutral expression.

"Yeah, she's my playmaker." Skyler's voice lowered, and he smirked, not hiding his admiration behind any pretense for one brief second before breaking eye contact and enthusiastically addressing the whole team. "Now let's go make some plays!"

The guys grunted their approvals with yeah! and let's go! and we all rose from our chairs and grabbed our pads and helmets.

As everyone shuffled out of the room, I caught Skyler's gaze, and he shrugged and winked at me. The tension had broken, and the rest of practice was fun and light. We could get through this.

CHAPTER SIXTEEN

Jonnie

"Aiden, will you go with me to the homecoming dance?" We were running together as we did every night, and I figured now would be as good a time as any. I didn't mean to make him trip over his own feet and do a faceplant.

Luckily Aiden is used to taking hits, but they're usually on the football field, not the jogging path.

"Are you okay?" I ran back and crouched beside him, trying to hoist him to a sitting position. Not an easy job. He may have trimmed down in recent weeks, but he was still a linebacker.

"I'm good." Aiden met my concerned gaze. "You just caught me off guard, that's all."

"Well, gee, if that's all it takes to knock a guy down, maybe I should ask out the entire defensive line on the opposing team."

"We'd win every game." Aiden hoisted himself to his feet and dusted himself off. "What made you decide to ask me?"

"Well, you and I jog together every night, and ya know, I'm pretty comfortable hanging out with you." We took off at a slower pace, one more conducive to holding a conversation.

"I kinda thought Jayce or Conner would have asked you by now," Aiden said.

"I don't know if either of them has figured out yet that there is a dance coming up."

"Were you hoping one of them was going to ask you to the dance?"

"Aiden, if I'd wanted one of them to ask me to the dance, would I have gone out of my way to ask you?" I turned and punched him in the arm, harder than I should have, but he didn't flinch. We just kept running.

"I just thought maybe I was a second"—he faked a cough into his hand—"or third choice. Like if one of them had asked you weeks ago, you wouldn't be asking me."

"Aiden, stop." I grabbed his arm, forcing him to a halt right there in the middle of the jogging path. "If I had wanted to go with one of them, I wouldn't have waited for them to get their heads out of their butts long enough to ask me. I would have asked them. But I didn't. I asked you."

"Okay, okay." He held his hands up in surrender. We continued our jog.

"I may have a little bit of ulterior motive in asking you," I admitted.

"I figured there was something," he said. "Lay it

on me."

"My mom always told me that if I ever got asked to a dance—which, prior to this year, was highly unlikely—I was required to go out with the first guy who asked me, otherwise it would be rude. I couldn't say no to the geeky kid in hopes that the hot guy would ask me."

"So, let me get this straight," Aiden said. "Am I the geeky kid or the hot guy?"

"You're neither." I realized my mistake immediately. "Oh! I didn't mean you weren't hot! You *totally* are! I just mean that I'm not choosing you for that kind of reason. I'm choosing you because I really like spending time with you. But also, because I don't want to encourage either of them."

"Okay, so you're choosing me to avoid choosing one of them?" By this time, we had finished our five-mile triangle and arrived back in front of my house. We stood in my driveway stretching and continuing our conversation.

"No, I chose you partially because I was afraid one of them was going to ask me," I said.

"And you would have had to say yes because they would have been the first guy to ask."

"Exactly."

He pursed his lips and lowered his brows, shifting his gaze away from mine. I pulled his arm around, so he'd look at me.

"But also because I enjoy spending time with you," I reminded him.

"But only as a friend?" Aiden asked.

"I don't want to mess up our friendship, if that's what you mean."

"Not entirely…"

I was afraid of this. "I'm not really in the right mindset to be more than friends with any of you right now." I bit my lower lip and averted my gaze.

"I figured as much." His tone of voice changed, and my head snapped up to meet his gaze.

"What do you mean by that?"

"He likes you too, you know?" Aiden raised his eyebrows.

"I-I don't know what"—I gulped—"I don't know what you mean."

"Yeah, right." Aiden snorted. "This is classic. The first time a girl asks me out, it's because she's trying to avoid being asked out by two other guys who like her because she likes a different guy who already has a girlfriend."

Before I could form a coherent answer, Aiden patted me on the shoulder and walked away chuckling.

"God, you have a sense of humor!" Aiden called into the sky, then turned, and spread his arms wide as he walked backward away from me. "Maybe I should be prepared with a nice handkerchief in my pocket to offer Amberlyn when she's crying on my shoulder after the dance."

"Very funny, Aiden," I called back to him.

"That's what I was thinking too," he mumbled and then called a little louder. "See ya at practice tomorrow."

CHAPTER SEVENTEEN

<u>Skyler</u>

"Hey, Aiden, I got you something at the mall yesterday," Jonnie said Monday morning. That caught my attention. What was Jonnie doing buying things for Aiden?

She and I, and Amberlyn, had just walked into the foyer by the gym where we hung out before school. Jonnie still caught a ride into school each morning. My daily dose of masochism.

The cheerleaders congregated in little groups with the volleyball players. The football players ogled both sets of girls and tried to pretend they weren't.

Jonnie pulled out a red and white polka dot bow tie. What the heck?

"That is so cool!" Aiden took the tie from Jonnie. "Does this match your dress?"

That got everyone's attention. Connor's jaw

dropped and Jayce asked, "What dress?"

"My homecoming dress," Jonnie said, batting her eyelashes at Jayce. *Why was my heart pounding?* Jonnie turned to Aiden, with a smile, and draped her arm through his. "Aiden and I are going to the homecoming dance together."

"What?" Connor had yet to close his mouth fully.

"How'd you swing that, bro?" Jayce asked.

"You lucky son of a jerk," Logan said.

Aiden's smirk seemed a little too… something. Satisfied? Secretive? Like he knew a secret the rest of us didn't. I narrowed my eyes at him when he raised his eyebrows at me. *What did she tell him?*

Amberlyn piped into the conversation. "I helped Jonnie pick out the *perfect* dress. She is going to look a-may-zing!"

"That must have been a fun shopping trip." Aiden's face remained passive even though I could tell he was forcing back a chuckle. I pressed my lips together, willing myself not to react.

"We had an awesome time," Jonnie said. After stepping away from Aiden, she draped her arm through Amberlyn's and pulled her in the direction of first hour. "Come on, let's get to class."

The rest of us followed behind the girls, half the guys on the team with crestfallen and confused looks on their faces. Aiden still wore a smirk as we pulled up to the rear of the group.

"Did Amberlyn buy you a pretty tie to go with *her* dress?" Aiden asked, draping his arm around my shoulder.

"Shut up, Aiden," I grumbled.

He laughed heartily but dropped his arm and patted me on the back and then headed down the hallway toward wood shop.

I was in deep trouble.

CHAPTER EIGHTEEN

<u>Jonnie</u>

Homecoming dinner at Gino's Pizza was fun for almost everyone. Amberlyn and Skyler had somehow pulled together half the cheerleading squad and half the football team into a huge group date, complete with pictures at the gazebo downtown.

All the parents had us line up with their cameras for group shots. I somehow managed to be squeezed in between Aiden and Skyler, almost as if they'd planned it that way. Or more like Aiden had planned it that way.

Aiden always pulled me into a position that, to make the group shot look right, made Skyler drape his arm around my back. Neither of us were complaining. Skyler even left his arm around my waist much longer than necessary for the shot. A couple times I felt his thumb move as if he was fighting the instinct to rub my back.

I wanted him to rub my back. I wanted him to pull me into his arms right there in front of the whole group and kiss me the way he'd almost kissed me two weeks ago.

My heart plummeted when Amberlyn's mom insisted that he stand with Amberlyn over by the elegant maple tree with the multi-colored leaves and positioned her and Skyler into various romantic shots. Him pinning on Amberlyn's corsage, her pinning on a boutonniere, him with his arms around her. I had to look away. I ran right into my date, Aiden.

"Hey," Aiden said, directing me away the maple tree. "My parents will probably want some shots with just the two of us." He wrapped his arm around my shoulders and almost cradled me against his body as if he was trying to comfort me. I fought the urge to cry and instead wrapped my arm around his waist.

"Thanks," I whispered. Aiden unexpectedly leaned over and kissed the top of my head. He was an incredible friend.

Amberlyn stood, cleared her throat, and raised her glass of pop, which yanked me out of the memory from an hour ago. "Can I have everyone's attention?"

We all turned, and conversation halted. Skyler sat beside Amberlyn, her hand on his shoulder as he played with the napkin beside his barely eaten slice of pizza.

"I'm so glad we could all come together tonight

for the homecoming dance!" She said it in her classic cheerleading voice as if she were giving a cheer rather than a toast. "I just want to say, congratulations to the football team for their fabulous win last night! Can they get a round of applause, guys?"

The girls all clapped and some of the guys cheered along as if *they* were the reason we'd won the night before. The real reason we'd won was because Skyler had thrown a million passes directly to me, and I'd run the ball what felt like hundreds of yards for dozens of touchdowns. My daydream was exaggerated, but not by much. We had been completely in sync all night.

Tonight, we should have had the same connection. Yet there he sat across the table, looking miserable, and here I sat cradled under the arm of my very perceptive and understanding date.

"I also want to thank my boyfriend, Skyler," Amberlyn continued. She paused and looked down at him with a loving smile and squeezed his shoulder. He raised his eyes to hers and smiled what I could tell was a fake smile. "This was his idea to get all of us together in a group, and I personally think it was a totally awesome idea."

"Yeah, way to go, Skyler," Logan called out, his arm draped around the back of the chair of a pretty blonde cheerleader. Skyler bumped fists across the table with Logan.

"The other part of his idea," Amberlyn said. "Was that all the guys in the group needed to make sure all the girls in the group never sat out a dance, unless they're tired of course. So, you boys make sure the girls don't get bored, okay?"

"I think we can accommodate you on that," Logan said with a smile. The little blonde cheerleader giggled and lowered her gaze.

The only guy I really wanted to dance with was already claimed. I felt no desire to attend the dance at all. I shoved my plate away and folded my arms in frustration.

CHAPTER NINETEEN

Skyler

The homecoming committee had transformed the gym into a starry night theme with hundreds of little white Christmas lights strung across the high ceiling. A silver disco ball spun in the middle of the room, casting sparkles everywhere.

True to their word, the guys had kept the ladies dancing all evening, mostly in a huge mosh group during the fast songs and pairing off during the slow songs. I had purposely steered clear of Aiden and Jonnie, not wanting to catch her eye while I was supposed to be dancing with my girlfriend. Girlfriend. What did that even mean anymore?

I let Amberlyn drag me back to our table to get a drink of her punch and found several other people milling around sitting at the table or standing nearby, including Jonnie and Aiden. I averted my gaze and waited with my hands in my pockets while Amberlyn gulped down several long swigs as if she was parched.

"I'm heading to the ladies' room," Amberlyn announced. "Anybody else need to go?"

"I do," one girl answered.

"I'll come too." Another girl hopped up, and the three of them headed off in a swish of fancy dresses, leaving just me, Aiden, and Jonnie at the table.

"What is it with girls all wanting to go to the restroom together?" Aiden asked playfully.

"I dunno," Jonnie answered. "I've never been a girl before."

I laughed so hard I snorted, and Aiden jumped in with the best come back line.

"Yeah, you went straight from tomboy to *woman*."

Did she ever. Tonight, in particular. I could barely remember that this elegant woman standing before me had caught five touchdown passes the night before. Was she even the same person?

Knowing Jonnie for years had skewed my vision of her. She was beautiful inside and out whether she was wearing grubby practice jerseys, a full uniform on a Friday night, shorts and a tank top at the beach, or a fancy polka-dotted dress that matched her date's bowtie.

The hair she'd chopped so short the day before preschool had grown into a golden mane that flowed down her back in curls during the school day, was pulled into a sloppy ponytail or braid for practices and games, and tonight was swept up and clipped in place with ribbons that accented her dress.

Oh my gosh. I'm in love with you. I almost said it out loud, right there in front of Aiden and anyone else who might be close enough to hear. The realization hit me like a punch to my gut. *I'm in love with Jonnie Gillis.*

Aiden cleared his throat, pulling me from my stupor. I forced my gaze over to him, and he raised his eyebrows. I couldn't even react, just allowed my focus to drift back toward Jonnie.

"I'm gonna go find some of those nachos." Aiden leaned over and kissed Jonnie's cheek. "I'm sure the two of you can find *something* interesting to talk about while I'm gone."

And just like that, Jonnie and I stood across from one another, almost alone, for the first time since the fateful night I'd almost kissed her. My heart raced, and my blood pounded in my ears.

As if just there to torment me, the song shifted to "Always" by Bon Jovi. I squeezed my eyes shut. This couldn't be happening to me. How was I supposed to stand across the table from the woman I had just determined I was in love with and pretend I didn't want her in my arms?

"Dance with me?" Was I asking or begging? I opened my eyes and met her gaze.

Before I knew what had happened, Jonnie was in my arms and we were somewhere in the darkest corner of the dancefloor, swaying to the beat of the most romantic love song that had ever been written by any songwriter as long as the world had been turning. I cursed Jon Bon Jovi for torturing me this way.

My body was pressed way too close to Jonnie's for anyone in that gym to pretend we were just friends. I couldn't pretend anymore.

But I had to.

I had to pretend that the silky feel of her form fitting dress didn't stir emotions inside of me. I had to pretend that heady coconut essence of her hair cascading down her face didn't tickle my nose, because of my cheek so close to hers. I had to pretend my heart wasn't pounding and my breathing hadn't increased. I had to pretend I wasn't in love with her.

As the song ended, we pulled further apart, and a less romantic song began. One calmer and quiet enough for us to have a conversation. My gaze bore into her, wishing I could convey what my heart was experiencing without words.

She was the first to break eye contact. Even though her voice was a mere whisper, I heard her as if she'd shouted in my ear. "Why haven't you broken up with her yet?"

"I don't know." I smoothed the tendrils of her hair back from her face, fighting the need to pull her close and press my lips to hers.

"Do you care about me?" Jonnie's voice hitched with unshed emotion.

"You know I do."

"Do I?" She pulled back, placing her hands on my chest. "Have you given me any reason to have hope?"

"What do you mean?" Panic pressed against my sternum.

"It's been *weeks*." Venom laced her words. "What are you waiting for?"

"I don't know," I said again.

"I don't want to be the other woman," she said, narrowing her eyes. "I don't want to be the eligible receiver standing in the end zone wide open and waiting for you to pass me the ball."

"You're not," I insisted. "You're so much more than that."

"I'm your playmaker. The one you throw Hail Mary passes to because you know she'll always be there." Her voice had risen and was gathering the attention of nearby students.

"Jonnie, lower your voice, please." I pleaded through clenched teeth.

"Why?" she asked much louder and pushed me away. "Are you afraid everyone will find out? I catch every—pass—you—throw."

With each word, she smacked me in the chest, and I moved back a step with each one, cowering as if she could actually hurt me. I let her take control of the conversation, wondering where she was going with this football analogy.

"I will *always* catch every pass you throw." She stepped closer and grabbed my tie, pulling me close and whispering, "Because I'm your playmaker."

Jonnie released my tie and shoved me backward.

"So, get your act together, *captain*." She spit the

words at me, turned with a swish of her polka-dotted dress, and called over her shoulder. "I'll see you on the *field*."

Jonnie walked purposefully through a parting sea of our classmates, straight over to a very stunned Aiden.

"Will you drive me home, please?" She turned and glared at me. "I've had enough of homecoming weekend."

CHAPTER TWENTY

Jonnie

"Jonnie!" Amberlyn pounced on my bed, jostling me awake from what little sleep I'd managed between crying and staring at the pictures on my phone.

Everyone in the school had posted homecoming weekend photos, and I tortured myself by scrolling through them on Instagram and Facebook. A few people had even sent me Snaps with cool shots from the game or the dinner or the dance.

Most photos were completely innocent. Others… not so much.

Someone had created a montage of photos involving me and Skyler. Him lifting me into the air while celebrating in the end zone after the winning touchdown. Him with his arm around me while in the lineup for photos at the gazebo, our heads close together while Amberlyn is talking to someone else, barely acknowledging her date. Him holding me on the dancefloor with our cheeks close together. That one was grainy and dark, barely recognizable other than my obvious polka-dotted dress and a clear shot of Skyler's face.

Videos had been posted of our argument, with captions like "Trouble in the end zone?" and "Has the winning streak come to an end?" and "What did Skyler do to anger his best receiver?"

Most photos and videos were complimentary toward me, my dress, my hair, my sexy calf muscles and three-inch heels, my touchdowns. They weren't necessarily uncomplimentary toward Skyler, rather more questioning, "What happened to break up the dream couple?"

None of them seemed to remember that Skyler and I weren't a couple.

Only one photo caption asked, "How does Amberlyn feel about Jonnie moving in on her man?"

I guess I was about to find out since she was yanking the covers off and bathing me with morning light streaking in the bedroom window. I moaned and tried to roll over.

"Jonnie, wake up! I want to hear all about your date with Aiden."

That caught my attention, and I sat straight up. *She didn't know?*

"Oh, sweetie, your poor face. Don't you know you can't sleep with makeup on?" Amberlyn climbed back off my bed and rushed into my adjoining bathroom, continuing her one-sided conversation. "I guess you wouldn't know that, would you? You've never worn makeup before now. Your mascara is smeared down your face as if you've been crying. You poor thing."

The faucet turned off, and Amberlyn squeezed water from a washcloth, then hurried back to my bed, and climbed up and over my mound of blankets, and kneeled next to me and wiped my face as if she were my mother, or as if I were her life-sized baby doll.

I looked up at her as she carefully removed the makeup that I had so carelessly allowed to remain on my skin as I cried myself to sleep. She had no clue. She hadn't heard any rumors. Or if she had, she was good at pretending she didn't know.

"I don't think I ever told you"—she pulled back with wide eyes—"Your dress was *perfect!* I mean, like, we outdid ourselves this time. And Aiden's tie! Oh my gosh, you guys looked *so* cute together. Have you seen the pictures all over social media? You are in just about all of them! No one can believe your transformation over the summer. We were right to curl your hair. You're so gorgeous. No wonder all the guys are in love with you."

Your boyfriend included, I almost said out loud. I sighed. She seriously didn't know. What was I going to do? I needed to tell her. "Yeah, so, about that…"

"Oh, I know everything," Amberlyn said, waving her hand in front of her as if she were shooing a fly.

"You do?"

"Oh, yeah, Skyler told me all about it."

"He did?" My heart pounded. "And you're okay with it?"

"Of course! That's why we got the whole group together," she said.

"Huh?" *I'm confused.*

"Yeah, Skyler told me the reason he needed to get all the guys from the football team to date the girls from the cheerleading squad was because all the guys were in love with you and it had become a distraction. I know all about that."

My shoulders fell. She knew nothing. We were back to square one. What was I going to do?

"You need to get in the shower," she said as if answering my unspoken question. "A bunch of us are going to get pedicures and after all that dancing, we need those foot massages. You're coming too, let's go." She pushed me gently but insistently off my bed.

Pedicure? I looked down at my ugly feet. I had never painted my toenails in my life. Still, if it involved a foot massage? I was totally down with that.

Shower first. I could get through this day.

CHAPTER TWENTY-ONE

<u>Skyler</u>

I wondered if Jonnie would find another ride to school on Monday morning, but she was right there with Amberlyn, her best friend and next-door neighbor. They climbed into my car, Amberlyn going on about some foot massage they'd had the day before.

"I wish we'd had them done on Saturday morning," she said as I was backing my car out of her driveway. "Because then we could have worn open-toed shoes to show off our nail polish. The color Jonnie picked out for hers would have perfectly matched her dress."

"You painted your toenails?" I caught Jonnie's reflection in the rearview mirror. I'm pretty sure I was asking Jonnie, but Amberlyn assumed I was asking her.

"Well, the nail tech actually does the toenail painting," Amberlyn said as she slipped off her little black flat and lifted her foot onto the glove compartment in a contorted position only a cheerleader could pull off. "See, aren't they beautiful?"

"Very nice," I said, barely glancing at them. I looked up into the rearview mirror. "You gonna show me your toenails also?"

"Not unless you want me to use them to kick you in places that will affect your ability to have children someday."

I cringed. "We wouldn't want that, now would we?"

She raised her eyebrows at me, and I winked at her. She lowered her gaze, drifting her focus toward Amberlyn.

Yeah, yeah, I know. I pulled my attention back to the road. I'd risked enough trouble already. How the heck was I supposed to break Amberlyn's heart? How badly was I breaking Jonnie's every day that I waited?

We pulled into the school parking lot and into my regular spot next to Logan, who had a new passenger. The blonde cheerleader from Saturday night was perched shotgun beside him. Amberlyn squealed and rushed from my car the minute I had the gear in park. I hadn't even turned off the engine.

I leaned my arms and forehead against the steering wheel and spoke quietly. "I'm sorry."

"Prove it."

"I will." My head lifted, and I met her gaze in the rearview mirror, taking advantage of the first time we'd spoken since our blow-up Saturday night. "One question, though. How?"

"How what?" Jonnie asked.

"How am I supposed to break up with her? You're her best friend. Give me some advice here."

"You want *my* advice on how to dump your girlfriend so that you can go out with me?"

"Umm… yes?" Was that the right answer? I raised my eyebrows.

"I don't know, either, Skyler." Jonnie sighed. "I tried to tell her yesterday, but she thought I was talking about all the other guys on the team. It's like she has no clue."

"Maybe we should just make out in front of her and see if she gets the picture."

"Tempting, but I don't think that would go over well." Jonnie fought a smile by biting her lower lip.

Man, I wanted to kiss her. "Okay, we've gotta get to class before I climb in that back seat with you and make out right now."

Jonnie had her hand on the door faster than I could think and I exited the car as well. Standing so close to one another, with a car between us and everyone else, I took her hand in mine briefly and gave it a quick squeeze. Whatever bodywash she used first thing in the morning, and after practice, wafted into my senses and nearly pulled me over the edge.

She held my gaze for three whole glorious seconds, then slowly released my hand, and stepped away, leaving me standing alone.

CHAPTER TWENTY-TWO

<u>Jonnie</u>

"Hey, Scrappy," Connor said as I approached the center of the field where the guys were gathering for practice. He stepped in front of Skyler, with his arms outstretched as if to protect him from me. "It is my job as offensive tackle to protect our quarterback at all costs, even if it's from our own players."

"Very funny, Connor." I rolled my eyes but caught the tiny smirk on Skyler's face and the way his eyebrows raised just slightly before he forced an expressionless mask. "I left my boxing gloves, and my evening gown, at home."

"Darn it," Jayce said, sidling up next to me and wrapping his arm around my waist. "I really, *really* liked that dress."

I could almost hear the growl from the back of Skyler's throat and saw the way his eyes narrowed at

Jayce.

"I'll let you borrow the dress if you like it so much." I bumped Jayce away with my hip. "I didn't realize that's what you were into."

"Ooh!" Connor taunted. "She got you."

"We can play dress-up together if that's what you want, babe." Jayce didn't take the hint that I was rejecting his advances, but I couldn't resist teasing him just a little bit more.

"So, you think just because I dress in guy's clothes"—I held up my football helmet—"That I like guys who dress up in girl's clothes?"

"Whatever turns you on, babe." Jayce raised his eyebrows.

"Okay, let's get started with practice," Skyler called out, a trace of anger in his voice. We all gathered closer and waited for instructions. "Most of you are going to run the perimeter of the field four times. Jayce, you and I are going to have a little chat. You too, Jonnie."

"Y'er in trouble," Connor said but took off at a decent pace. The other guys chuckled or shook their heads or patted Jayce on the shoulder as they started off down to the end of the field. Aiden led the pack. What a change from the first day of practice. I couldn't help smiling.

Skyler cleared his throat after everyone else was out of earshot. "Jayce, I know you think it's funny to make suggestive comments to Jonnie, but I doubt she welcomes your advances."

"She knows I'm joking," Jayce said, wrapping his

arm around my shoulder. "We've been poking fun at each other for years."

"Well, I've noticed your *joking* has become a little more inappropriate, and I don't think any of us want a sexual harassment charge on our high school transcripts. Am I right?"

Jayce dropped his arm from around my shoulder and stepped away from me. "Dude, not cool to say crap like that."

"Jayce, you know I'm not gonna make that kinda claim, but Skyler's right," I said.

"Woah, can I hear you say that again?" Skyler put his hand to his ear. "Did you just say, 'Skyler's right'?"

"Whatever." I pushed Skyler's shoulder and fought the desire to wrap my arms around his waist.

"I'm sorry if I made you feel uncomfortable, Jonnie." Jayce lowered his gaze and shuffled his cleat against the turf.

"I'm fine, seriously." I wrapped my arms around Jayce. Funny how it was okay to give a hug to the guy I *didn't* like but not okay to hug the guy I was in love with.

Woah, did I just think that? Was I in love with Skyler? My jaw gaped as I caught Skyler's gaze, but I shook it off and continued what I needed to say to Jayce. I shifted so I could look up at the hunky lineman beside me. "But you need to know that I'm *not* interested in you as more than a friend. I hope we can go back to the way we were back when I was flat chested and had short hair."

Skyler choked on the water he was drinking, and I bit my lips to keep from laughing. It was kind of fun to have such an effect on Skyler. He sputtered for a moment and coughed a few times, but Jayce ignored him.

"Yeah, I kinda figured you weren't interested in me about the time you asked Aiden to the homecoming dance," Jayce said.

"That really made a statement, didn't it?"

"So, is he, like, your boyfriend now?" Jayce asked. Now it was my turn to cough and sputter.

"Um, no, we just like hangin' out," I said, clearing my throat. "I don't currently have a boyfriend." I glared at Skyler, and he narrowed his eyes at me. Thankfully Jayce didn't seem to notice our exchange.

"I think it's time we get warmed up," Skyler said, stretching his hamstrings. "Run the perimeter with me?"

I wished Skyler was talking to just me, but unfortunately Jayce took off at a casual pace with us. Was Skyler purposefully running this slow? We fell into step about five feet behind the rest of the pack.

Jayce instinctively started racing rather than running. He was a track star in the spring, like me, but with a much more competitive spirit. Within less than a minute, he had pushed past the rest of the team.

"You know what I like about football practice?" Skyler asked. I suspected I knew his answer already. "I get to be with you, and no one questions it."

"We get to run together like we've done for

years," I said in agreement.

"Exactly."

We settled into our usual pace in companionable silence.

CHAPTER TWENTY-THREE

<u>Jonnie</u>

"I'm telling you, number forty-five is targeting Jonnie!"

"That's the cornerback's job, Skyler," Logan said. "To guard the wide receiver. Ours does the same thing."

"But he's taking it too far." Skyler pointed across the field in exasperation. Our thirty-second timeout was almost over and Skyler had been ranting the whole time.

"Skyler, I'll be fine," I told him. "You just get me the ball and I'll take it from there." My fingers were freezing standing around like this. We needed to get moving.

"Fine," Skyler grumbled. He called the play, and we ran back onto the field.

He was right, of course, but I didn't want to admit

I was afraid. Their cornerback was huge and fast. And handsy. He wasn't afraid to reach around for the ball even if it meant grabbing hold of me like he would any other guy. Most defensive players shied away from guarding me as thoroughly as they should, probably in fear they'd grab parts that shouldn't be touched.

I got into position, knowing I'd most likely be the decoy this play unless Doug couldn't get open. I still needed to be ready.

I ran hard and fast but forty-five kept up with me. There was no way for me to get open. Skyler would have to seek other options.

The whistle blew, and the chain gang started moving the chains. Logan had run for fifteen yards before I could even turn around to see what had happened.

Skyler must have changed the play at the last second because that wasn't supposed to be a running play. Doug was the intended receiver. Period. If Doug couldn't get open, the ball was heading my way.

For the next play, I was set up for a hook, but I thought Doug was the target again. The next thing I knew, Jayce had the ball and he picked up another first down. I should have been satisfied we were moving the chains down the field. Instead I had a disconcerting suspicion I was being purposefully kept out of the line of communication.

After another two plays where things didn't go the way I thought they were planned, I called Skyler on it.

"What's your deal, Skyler?" I practically growled into the huddle, fighting the desire to scream at him but not wanting the whole stadium to hear my frustration. "Are you gonna tell me the real play this time? Or are you all going to keep me in the dark."

"You weren't the intended receiver," Skyler said. "End of story."

"How am I supposed to protect myself if I don't know what the rest of you are doing out there?"

"You could go sit on the bench and let one of the freshmen get some playing time," Skyler suggested, narrowing his eyes. I narrowed mine right back.

"Dude, she's right, man." Connor shoved Skyler's shoulder. "We all need to be on the same page."

"Fine. You want the ball, Gillis? You got it. Set up your hook, get away from forty-five and get open."

"Fine," I said. We broke the huddle and set up my favorite trick play. True to my word, I was open, and for the first time in the whole second quarter, the ball landed in my hands.

Just as I turned to run up the field, their cornerback hit me so hard the ball flew from my hands, and I crashed to the ground. Jayce dove on the ball, and we recovered our own fumble without a loss of yardage.

That didn't stop Skyler from getting into forty-five's face and challenging him with a few choice swear words and accusations of targeting. Whistles blew, flags were thrown, and before we could gather ourselves back to the line of scrimmage, we'd been charged with a fifteen-yard penalty and a warning for our quarterback.

"Ref, that was *clearly* targeting!" Skyler yelled. "No touchdown is worth a player's safety!"

Logan pulled Skyler away from the defensive back and chastised him away from my range of hearing, helmet to helmet like two deer with antlers locked. A little guy-to-guy pep talk, helping Skyler down from his rage. Logan was a good friend. He smacked him on the helmet, and they all ran back into position.

Skyler's temper tantrum cost us the lead going into the half, and everyone was angry as we headed to the locker rooms, not that I had the honor of participating in that tirade. I stomped into the girls' locker room and seethed while my team yelled at each other on the other side of a concrete barrier. Not even the cheerleaders joined me. I was alone.

CHAPTER TWENTY-FOUR

<u>Skyler</u>

"What was that mess I just witnessed?" Coach Bryant threw his clipboard to the floor of the locker room. "Who gave you authority to change the plays at the last second and not tell your receivers?"

"It's *my* call when I'm out there looking around at the defensive lineup and decide to change!" I yelled right back, knowing I was risking retribution if I talked back to coach.

"It is *not* your call if you don't pass the message all the way down the line!" Coach stepped around the bench that was anchored to the cement floor with bolts.

My cleats found no resistance as I backed away, thinking coach was going to shove me into the lockers, but I barely lessened my tone. "The message got as far as it needed to get."

"You kept your receiver in the dark during key plays at a time when she was being threatened by the opponent!"

His massive form hulked over me, and fire sparked behind his eyes.

"I was trying to *protect* her!" I yelled.

"You left her *defenseless*," coach accused. I cringed at his choice of words.

"No…" My voice wavered. "I was—I was trying to protect her."

"By keeping her in the dark, you made her more vulnerable." Coach Bryant took two steps back and shook his head with disgust.

"You need to take her out." I pointed out the door. "You need to bench her. That guy is too big, too fast. She's gonna—she's gonna get hurt…" My voice trailed off, and I stumbled, my back against the wall of blue and gold lockers, the entire team staring at me, helmets in hand, covered in mud and grass stains.

If a cornered puppy dog could have donned a football jersey and pads, that would have been me.

Aiden smirked and shook his head. "Dude, when are you finally going to admit it out loud?"

I kept my mouth shut. There was no correct answer to that question. My eyes darted around the room, never locking gazes with any of them.

"Ah, man, seriously?" Connor asked.

"Not that I blame you, dude," Jayce said. "She is smokin' hot."

"It's not like that," I choked out. "She's my best friend."

"Best friend with benefits," Doug mumbled.

"I would *never.*" I started after Doug, but Logan stepped in and held me back.

"Sky, dude, come on." Logan had me by the shoulders and pulled me away from Doug. His voice was calm, soothing. "We're on your side, man. You're our brother.

We're here for you."

"Does Amberlyn know?" Jayce asked.

"That is none of your business, Jayce," I yelled, agitated more. Logan pulled me back again. I didn't fight him.

"We're not gonna deal with that right now," Logan said, locking eyes with me. "The only thing we can help you with over the next hour is to get you through this game. What you choose to do after that is *not our concern*."

Logan turned his head to Jayce and glared at him. Jayce was the first to look away.

I tried to slow my breathing and stop my body shaking. The locker room packed with sweaty, muddy football players was pressing against me from all sides. I stepped over to the adjoining restroom and splashed water on my face and stared at myself in the mirror.

I knew Logan was right. I needed to calm down and get through this game. After that, it was time to make some changes. I couldn't put this off any longer. But we had a more immediate problem. I pulled myself together, squared my shoulders and confidently entered the locker room again.

"What are we going to do about forty-five?" I growled.

CHAPTER TWENTY-FIVE

<u>Jonnie</u>

The guys all had strange expressions when they exited the locker room. I knew I must look a mess, with mud and grass covering my clothes and my hair falling out of its braid, but some of them seemed almost angry. *What did I do?*

Defeated, they shuffled out one by one, helmets in hand, glanced at me, and either shook their heads or chuckled. Then they shoved their helmets on their heads and ran onto the field. When Aiden walked out, he strode right over to me and pulled me into his arms.

A hug? During a football game? What the heck? He released me with a grin, put on his helmet, and ran onto the field.

Skyler was the last guy out of the locker room, and he trudged over to me, a resigned expression. His eyes searched my face and for a moment I thought he was going to kiss me. Instead, he pulled me into an embrace, holding his helmet in his right hand so it bumped against my back.

"Sorry I lost my temper, babe." His choked near whisper contained more emotion than I'd heard him express since I yelled at him during the homecoming dance.

I wasn't sure how to respond so I just wrapped my arms around him, my helmet bumping against his back.

"They all know," Skyler said. He was still holding me. I was aware that where we stood, the whole stadium could see us, should anyone be paying attention.

"I didn't say anything to anyone." I pulled back in a panic, wondering if he was mad at me. "I mean, Aiden sorta figured it out, but I didn't tell him."

"No, no, it wasn't you." He shook his head and lowered his gaze. "They can just tell."

"What are you going to do?" I asked, shaking with a mixture of dread and excitement.

"I guess I'm gonna have a talk after the game with my soon-to-be ex-girlfriend."

"I'm sorry," I said. "That's gonna be a tough conversation."

"You have nothing to be sorry about." He held my gaze, took a deep breath, and squared his shoulders. "And it's long overdue."

"Come on," I said, looking across the field at the clock, less than thirty seconds until halftime was over. "Let's go finish this game, and we'll deal with the rest later."

We both donned our helmets and ran together over to our sideline where the rest of the team waited. The huddle opened to make space for us, and Skyler looked up to Coach Bryant. "Your team, coach."

"That was a tough first half, but it's time to move forward," coach said. "We're gonna take the high road on this, right?"

There were nods of agreement around the huddle and some grumbling.

"If there's an issue with targeting, I will calmly speak to the refs, and there will be no more fighting. Is that clearly understood?"

"Yes, sir," Skyler mumbled, chastised. The rest of the team nodded in assent.

"Your team, captain." Coach Bryant stepped back, and the huddle closed the gap.

"You heard coach," Skyler said. "I'm sorry I lost my temper, but I will not let my team be targeted. I will also not back down or be bullied. This is our field, our home turf. We own this field. Now let's go out there and show them what it means to own this field!"

We received the kickoff and took the field, Skyler offering one more last huddle for just the offense.

"Logan and Jayce, take out forty-five and get a hole open for Jonnie. While she's running for the end zone, I'm gonna fake to Doug and then throw a Hail Mary to Jonnie. By the time their cornerback gets free from Logan and Jayce—and he will; he's bigger than both of you combined—she'll be far enough downfield that he won't be able to catch up, not enough to target her anyway. The rest of you, guard me as if your life depends on it so I can hold the ball long enough for Jonnie to get down the field."

We broke huddle and lined up in a split screen formation. The trick play Skyler had decided on was risky, but we had revenge and retaliation on our side. Doug and I flanked Skyler equidistant on either side, lending no clues which of us was the target. Because Skyler had been avoiding me during the first half, the defense wouldn't necessarily assume I'd be the intended receiver.

The play started off fine. I relied on my blockers to hold the defensive cornerback long enough for me to get past, and they did. I flew down the field, knowing forty-five would be hot on my heels. At the five-yard line, I hooked toward center, trusting the ball would be at my shoulder at exactly... the... perfect... moment.

Skyler's aim was perfect. My run was perfect. My catch was perfect. A few more steps to the end zone. My heart pounded as I raced that last few yards, not turning back to see if the cornerback was on my heels. I just ran. Two yards. One yard. Touchdown!

My heart soared. We'd done it! We'd gotten past him, and I'd caught a thirty-yard Hail Mary against the odds!

As I spiked the ball in celebration, I was hit from behind by a truck.

The world went black.

CHAPTER TWENTY-SIX

<u>Skyler</u>

"Touchdown!" My hands raised in a goal-post celebration as the girl I loved caught the perfect pass I'd thrown and ran five more yards into the end zone, with number forty-five hot on her heels. She didn't even seem nervous.

Just as she spiked the ball in celebration, the enormous cornerback hit her from behind, with all the momentum and force of a freight train.

She hit the ground and didn't move.

"Jonnie!"

I ripped my helmet off as I ran, desperate to reach her. The field was in pandemonium as coaches and referees and players rushed forward.

The refs had no excuse this time. The call was obvious from the other side of the stadium. Targeting. Forty-five was ejected from the game. A little late now! I wanted to scream at that referee. I wanted to beat the tar out of that bully. I wanted to get to my Jonnie.

Never had thirty-five yards seemed so long. My legs were pulling through molasses for how slow they were moving.

Several other players and one referee had reached her before me and were crouched or knelt by her side. I wanted to push them out of the way so I could get to her.

"Is she okay?" I fell to my knees near her head, where she lay still, her helmet on, and her left arm tucked under her in an unnatural position. The only comfort in her being unconscious was that she couldn't feel that dislocated shoulder—yet.

No one dared move her in case she had a neck injury, until the team doctors from both sides of the field arrived. They rolled her carefully onto a board while stabilizing her head and neck.

I was vaguely aware of Logan's arms, and other players around me, and Aiden quietly praying somewhere nearby, and ambulance sirens, and people everywhere, and Jonnie's mom and dad, and people rushing around, and the Gator rushing forward, and Jonnie being lifted onto the back, and the team and I running after it to meet the ambulance at the back gate.

The medics had her onto a gurney in mere seconds, and I could no longer see her as they turned to wheel her away.

"Jonnie!" I called out in one last ditch effort to

somehow reach her.

"Skyler," a weak voice cried.

I rushed forward past the coaches and team doctors to her right side so I wouldn't jostle her left shoulder. "I'm here, babe. I'm right here."

"Did you see my touchdown?" Somehow her little weak voice held a smile.

"Yeah, babe, I saw it." I reached for her hand and leaned forward and kissed her lips over and over, desperately, clinging to her hand. "I saw your touchdown."

"I'm your playmaker," she whispered, and cringed. "Don't you forget it."

"You'll always be my playmaker, babe." I kissed her again. "Always."

"Okay, man, we gotta get her to the hospital," one of the paramedics insisted. "I need you to step back."

"I love you, Jonnie." I kissed her one more time before someone pulled me back, and I stumbled. Someone held me up as my knees buckled, Logan? Aiden, maybe? I didn't care. I was just glad they were there for me. As I tried to stand, I knew I couldn't drive on my own. I choked out a request. "Somebody get me to the hospital."

We turned around to see two cheerleaders on either side of Amberlyn, holding her as tears ran down her face.

Oh crap.

CHAPTER TWENTY-SEVEN

<u>Skyler</u>

Amberlyn rushed forward and threw herself into my arms, crying hard. "Is Jonnie going to be okay, Skyler? I'm so scared."

I wrapped my arms around her tentatively. In some strange natural transition, I was comforting Jonnie's best friend rather than my former girlfriend.

"I hope so," I choked out, lowering my face until my cheek rested against her head. I didn't know what else to say. I whispered, "I'm sorry."

"Can I come with you to the hospital?" Amberlyn pulled away and looked up at me, her brow creased and tears streaking her makeup. I wiped her cheeks, knowing she'd be mortified if she could see herself in a mirror. "We can talk, ya know, about everything else later."

I tried to smile, but my face was probably more of a grimace, pained and remorseful. My voice was horse when I could finally speak. "Of course."

"I'll drive," Aiden said, patting me on the shoulder. "Let's go get our pads off first, okay?"

"That's probably a good idea." I pulled away and disentangled myself from Amberlyn.

"I'll go grab my purse and tell my coach where I'm going," Amberlyn said. "I'll meet you outside the locker room."

The game had resumed with mostly second-string players. Aiden and Logan flanked me and helped me find my way to the locker room.

It was too much. It was all too much. My girlfriend had just witnessed me confessing my love to, and kissing, another girl, who was in an ambulance racing to the hospital for an injury that could have been prevented if I had insisted that she not play.

I pulled my jersey over my head and practically ripped my pads from my shoulders and pulled my jersey back on, not bothering with a shower and change of clothes. I barely took the time to change out of my cleats. Aiden did the same, and within three minutes, we were back out of the locker room and found Amberlyn waiting.

Another person was waiting nearby. A sullen face I didn't recognize because he'd hid behind a helmet that he now held in his hand. He was large enough to play college ball, and his jersey read 45. I couldn't believe we ever let Jonnie play opposite him. What were we thinking?

I stepped closer to him and had to raise my chin to look him in the eye. I didn't flinch. "You have a lot of nerve showing up here."

"I'm sorry, man. I really am." He sounded remorseful but still with a hint of cockiness behind his demeaner as if that was his natural expression.

"It's too late for sorry." I spit my words at him. "You'd better pray she's okay, or so help me—" Before I could finish my sentence, Aiden had me by the shoulders and turned me toward the parking lot.

"Come on, Sky, let's go." Aiden dragged me along, but I hollered over my shoulder.

"I hope you have a good attorney!"

"Skyler, come on. Let's get to Jonnie." Amberlyn's voice and Jonnie's name pulled me back from my fury, and I allowed myself to be dragged along toward Aiden's car.

The emergency room was already packed by the time we got there. Friday night was not a great time for an injury. We rushed to the receptionist desk, and before she could ask how she could help, I blurted out, "My girlfriend was just brought by ambulance. I need to know if she's okay."

"I'm sorry," the receptionist said. "Only family is allowed back there. You'll have to wait until one of her family comes out to give you more information."

"But—but she's my, my Jonnie. I need to know she's okay."

"I'm sure her family will let you know as soon as

they have some news. Now go have a seat and someone will be with you shortly."

"Come on, Skyler," Aiden said, dragging me away from the receptionist. He helped me to a seat in the far corner, and I slumped over, squeezing my eyes shut and pulling at my sweaty mess of hair.

I should have showered before we'd left.

I should have known they wouldn't let me back to see her.

I should have insisted she sit on the bench.

I should have thrown the ball to Doug.

I should have told her I loved her a long time ago.

I should have broken up with my girlfriend the minute I realized I was in love with Jonnie.

I should have told her how beautiful she looked in that dress.

"Skyler?"

I jumped, startled to see Amberlyn's concerned face. She sat next to me, with her hand on my knee.

"She'll be okay, Skyler." Amberlyn's voice was soothing. "She wouldn't have been able to talk to you if she wasn't at least a little bit okay."

"I shouldn't have let her play against that guy." I shook my head back and forth slowly.

"You can't blame yourself," she said, smoothing the creases on my forehead.

"I'm sorry I didn't break up with you." I heard the vulnerability in my own voice. She sat back in her chair and dropped her hands to her lap.

"We're having that conversation already, huh?" She lowered her gaze.

"We shoulda had it a long time ago."

"How long has this been…"

"Since Preschool?" I chuckled sheepishly. She looked up at me, and her jaw dropped. "I'm kidding. Sort of."

"You know what's funny?" Amberlyn smiled. "I kinda thought you were gay?"

"What?" I couldn't hide a grin. "Why?"

"Well, you never really made a move on me the whole time we were dating."

"I respect you too much for that." I held Amberlyn's hand gently in mine and realized something. "You know, this is gonna take some getting used to."

"What is?" she asked. I raised our interlinked hands.

"Not holding your hand and stuff. We've been together for so long, it just kinda comes naturally."

"I have a feeling you'll be holding someone else's hand pretty soon."

"Is that gonna be weird for you?" I raised my eyebrows.

"Nah." She bumped her shoulder against mine. "Just don't go makin' out with her in front of me, 'kay?"

"I'll try my best not to." I chuckled.

"Seriously though, how long has this been going on?"

"I think when she got back from visiting her dad and all the guys started flirting with her, I got super jealous. She's always been *my* Jonnie, not theirs."

"Possessive much?"

"You know what I mean." I squeezed my hand around hers. "We've been buds, best friends, teammates, for as long as I can remember. You nailed it a month ago."

"What do you mean?" She creased her brow.

"You said, 'If your best friend is a girl, doesn't that make her your girlfriend?' and I scoffed at the notion."

"I had been right." She sat up straighter and smiled.

"Thank you…" I said softly.

"For what?" Amberlyn asked, lowering her gaze.

"You just watched me *kiss* your best friend, and, and…"

"Yeah, I know."

"And you didn't even slap me in the face or anything."

"The night is still young," she said, a tiny grin creeping onto her face.

"You have been an amazing girlfriend."

"And you've been an amazing boyfriend."

"Thank you," I said again.

There was commotion in the doorway as Coach Bryant and several other players and cheerleaders and schoolmates and teachers and family gathered in the foyer. Amberlyn, Aiden, and I hurried over.

"I spoke with Jonnie's mom," coach said, holding up his hands to quiet the crowd. "They think she has whiplash and a mild concussion. Oh, and a dislocated shoulder."

"She's gonna be okay," I whispered. My statement was almost a question, almost a relieved sigh. Coach patted my cheek. My shoulders relaxed.

"Yeah, buddy. I think she's going to be okay."

"Can I see her?"

"They're going to keep her overnight for observation and to get her stabilized. Once they get her settled into a room, one or two of us will probably be allowed to quickly say goodnight. But she's going to need to rest." Coach looked around at everyone gathered. "We all need to rest. Why don't you all go home and see her when she's feeling better?"

"I'm not leaving until I've seen her," I said definitely.

"I figured you'd say that," coach said. "I planned to wait with you."

"Thank you," I choked out, grateful for my mentor.

"I'll get Amberlyn home," Aiden said.

"She's my best friend." Amberlyn clung to my arm. "I don't want to leave either."

"It could be hours, babe. You need to get some rest." I pulled her close and kissed her forehead. "I'll tell Jonnie you were here and that you'll come back in the morning, okay?"

"Okay," she squeaked out. She gave me one last hug and slipped from my arms.

I sighed as my now-former girlfriend walked away, clinging to the arm of my best defensive lineman. Interesting.

When I turned back around, my coach had his eyebrows raised. "This evening has been... enlightening." He cocked his head to the side. "So, you and Jonnie, huh? I never saw that coming."

"Shut up. You're such a liar." I shook my head. "You probably knew before I did."

"I had a hunch," coach said. "You had to figure it out for yourself."

"Yeah, I guess I did."

We sat and waited, mostly silent, for almost two hours.

CHAPTER TWENTY-EIGHT

<u>Jonnie</u>

"Hi, Skyler," my mom said softly. My ears perked up. From where she was seated by the window, my mom could see the door to my hospital room, but my neck was held in place with a firm collar. The ever-present scent of antiseptic clung to every fiber of the thin blankets covering my body. "You can't stay long. She needs rest."

"I just wanna say hello." Skyler's husky voice sounded tired and worried. He barely pushed the curtain aside and slipped close to my bed. My right hand reached for his, and he grasped it as if I were a lifeline, giving him strength. "Hey, babe, how you feelin'?"

"Like I got hit by a truck." My hoarse whisper pushed through my groggy mind. "How 'bout you?"

"Like my girlfriend got hit by a truck."

"What a coincidence."

He leaned forward and pressed his lips very softly to mine. "I'm so glad you're okay."

"Who told you that lie?" I asked, clearing my throat, trying to pull humor from thin air. "I got hit by a truck, remember?"

"Too well," he said, creasing his brow. He was still covered in sweat and dried mud.

"You need a shower."

"Do I smell that bad?" His eyes sparkled, probably relieved that I was able to make jokes.

My mom cleared her throat. "Hey, guys, I'm going to run to the ladies' room real quick. Do you think you'll be okay in here for a few minutes?" She didn't wait for us to answer, just snuck out the door, with a chuckle. I turned my attention back to Skyler.

"I was pretty out of it earlier," I said, thinking how much I still was out of it with all the pain killers they'd given me. Before I lost the nerve, I asked the question I'd been wondering about. "Did I imagine that you told me you loved me?"

"No, you didn't imagine that." His eyes searched mine.

"Is it true?" I asked. He nodded slowly, seriously. "Do you think, maybe, you could say it again, ya know, since I'm kinda awake now?"

"I love you," Skyler whispered.

"I love you too," I whispered. "Did you break up with your other girlfriend yet?"

"She kinda dumped me when she saw me kissing you."

"Oh no! Are you okay?"

"Jonnie, I'm teasing." He brought his face back to mine and kissed me again. "She's actually really worried about you. She came with me to the hospital."

I glanced toward the door, excited to see my best friend.

"Nah, everyone else went home to bed. She wanted me to tell you that she'll come see you tomorrow morning when you're feeling better."

"Why are you still here?"

"I refused to leave until they let me see you."

"What time is it?"

"One-thirty," he said.

"It's past your bedtime, young man," I scolded, my own bedtime had long since come and gone. "You need to go home and get some sleep."

"I told you, I refused to leave until I saw you."

"You've seen me now you can go home," I said, my own eyes growing heavy but regretting telling him to go home the minute the words slurred from my mouth. "Can you do me a favor first? Will you stay with me until I fall asleep?"

"Of course," he whispered. As my eyes closed, his lips met mine one more time. I turned my face toward him and rested my forehead against his.

"I expect there to be a lot more kisses from now on," I mumbled as I drifted away.

Somewhere nearby I heard Skyler's voice. *Goodnight, Jonnie. I love you.*

I smiled. *I love you too, Skyler.*

CHAPTER TWENTY-NINE

<u>Skyler</u>

The doctors wouldn't let Jonnie go back to school until the following Friday. I visited her every day after practice. She grilled me on plans and plays and techniques, wanting to know what the team was going to do without her this Friday night, as if this was the only Friday night they had to worry about.

Her eventual return to football was a touchy subject. I was torn between my need to protect her and my desire to connect with her on the field again. I didn't want to get her hopes up, or mine.

I knew we needed to treat her just as we would a guy who had gotten hurt on the football field. How long would he have to sit out? A few plays? The rest of the game? What would be the process of him returning to the game? A quick run through of concussion protocol? Make sure he was able to maintain mental faculties? Pop that shoulder back into place? Maybe a few weeks of physical therapy? I had to push aside my protective instinct as her boyfriend.

Her boyfriend.

That was so cool. I was Jonnie Gillis's boyfriend. The inevitability had been obvious since we were little kids. Running around at all hours of the day, playing every sport imaginable, eating popsicles, and wrestling.

Wrestling. I chuckled. Our parents probably wouldn't approve of that now.

As it was, we'd probably get in trouble for the way we were lying on the couch watching Netflix, our legs intertwined and her head in the crook of my arm, snuggled so close I could smell that amazing shampoo and body wash, and okay, I needed to get off the couch now.

Darn it. Why do I torture myself this way? I shrugged out from under her and shoved myself to the other side of the couch. Just to be on the safe side I climbed over to the Lazyboy chair. I finally just decided to go home.

The little vixen was lying over there laughing at me. "Are you gonna pick me up for school tomorrow?"

"Of course." I leaned down to kiss her goodbye and had to force myself not to climb back onto that couch and stay for the rest of the… movie. The rest of the movie. Yeah, that's exactly what I was thinking. "Goodbye, Jonnie."

"See ya in the morning, Skyler." She kept laughing as I headed out to my car.

CHAPTER THIRTY

Jonnie

"Do I get to sit in the front seat?" I grinned with teasing admiration as Amberlyn held open the passenger side door for me to climb into Skyler's Ford Fusion.

"You won him fair and square," she said, a twinkle in her eye.

"Very funny, you two," Skyler said. "Now get in the car before we make ourselves late for school.

They'd both been over at my house several times that week at the same time and everything felt perfectly natural. We were just three friends hanging out. In a lot of ways, it was more comfortable than when the two of them had been dating because our lives were at balance.

Amberlyn and Skyler were never meant to be a couple. Theirs had been a relationship of convenience. Someone to hang out with and hold hands with and stake a claim on so that when other girls thought of flirting with Skyler, he was always off-limits. He belonged to Amberlyn. Except he never really had. He had belonged to me all along. And I'd belonged to him. We belonged together.

Still, riding to school in the front seat of his car was different. I turned around and saw my best friend sitting behind me, and we grinned at each other. "This is so weird."

"Hey, you guys, did I tell you that Aiden asked me to go to the movies with him on Saturday?" Amberlyn pulled herself forward and hung her face over the back of my seat. "Is that going to be weird for either of you?"

"Nope," Skyler and I answered at the same time.

"He's my second favorite guy on the football team," I said, grinning over at Skyler. "I haven't been able to go running with him in over a week. He's probably enjoying your company."

"He's a good guy, Amberlyn." Skyler told her. "You'll have fun together."

"He's excited for baseball season to start," she said.

"Don't you mean basketball?" I asked.

"No, Aiden said he goes to the batting cage a few times a week, and he's hitting really well. He takes private lessons year-round."

"You probably didn't realize that," Skyler said, turning his face slightly toward me. "Because you're so focused on track season each spring. Aiden's a really good baseball player. He'll probably have recruiters at his games."

"Really? That's so cool."

Conversation was light and easy as Skyler drove, and we arrived in our usual parking spot. Instead of walking along with Amberlyn and Skyler holding hands, Skyler wrapped his arm around my waist as we walked in side by side.

We were both wearing our football jerseys because it was Friday and we always dressed in jerseys on Fridays before games. I wouldn't be in full gear that evening, but I would be on the sidelines beside my team.

I wore a loose sling to school that day, still babying my shoulder. The sling was more of a reminder to be careful, and for others to steer clear of that side. On Monday I would resume practice and by Friday of next week, if all went well and I showed no additional symptoms, I would be back on the field.

In the space of one week my life had changed. No, over the past thirteen years my life had changed.

CHAPTER THIRTY-ONE

<u>Jonnie</u>

I walked in the point position this time, trying to make a statement. The opposing team had capitalized on home field advantage and were already in uniform and ready to start warm-ups. Our team had just stepped off the bus, and we were still in our dress clothes.

The opposing team turned in our direction, with wide eyes as we stood before them. My miniskirt was just slightly longer than the cheerleaders and my cashmere sweater hugged every curve. A couple of the guys looked me up and down, and I raised my eyebrows. They backed down.

"I'm sure you've all heard what happened two weeks ago," I started, my hand on my hip. "I'm all better now, so I expect you guys to treat me like any other wide receiver. Got it?"

Several of the guys nodded or grunted. One said yes ma'am in a very respectful tone. Another said whatever. I could tell they were trying not to let me intimidate them.

"I'm not afraid of you, so don't be afraid of me. I will respect you if you need to tackle me; I can hold my own. Under *normal* football game conditions, I can hold my own. Besides, if you do try anything, my boyfriend will not hesitate to retaliate."

"And good luck figuring out which one of us is her boyfriend since we all protect her like we are," Jayce said. I smiled over at him.

"Yeah right," one of the guys on their team said, snorting. "We've all seen the YouTube videos of your quarterback crying and falling all over you."

"I was not crying," Skyler said with a hint of smirk. "Quarterbacks don't cry."

"Whatever," the opponent said. "As captain of the Rockford High team, you have my word that there will be no targeting from my guys. We will beat you fair and square." He extended his hand, and I shook it with firm respect.

"We look forward to proving you wrong," I said. Then we shook hands all around each other's teams, and we headed to the locker rooms.

I enjoyed walking hand in hand with our quarterback.

"Cried, huh?" I nudged my shoulder against his. "I kinda wish I'd been awake to see that."

"Shut up, I did not cry," Skyler said.

"He cried." Logan hid his accusation behind a

fake cough.

I laughed and wrapped my arms around Skyler. "I would have cried if you'd gotten hurt too."

"Come here, you little vixen." Skyler diverted me away from the entrance to the locker rooms, where we would have to separate to change into our uniforms.

The other guys called jeers and taunts and made fake kissing noises as Skyler pulled me into the relative privacy beside the building. We probably within sight of quite a few people, but I didn't care.

With my back pressed against the rough concrete exterior of the building, I pulled Skyler by his shirt to bring him close.

Just to torment me, he placed one hand on the concrete beside my head and, with the other, pulled his fingers down the length of my long, blonde hair. His husky voice teased me more than his words. "I love your hair down like this."

"You usually only see me with a helmet on and my hair in a braid or scrunchy."

"Football season's nearly over," he said. "Will you wear it down more often? Just for me?"

"Now that I'm a girl, you mean?"

"You're not a girl, Jonnie." Skyler leaned very close, almost to where his lips were touching mine. "Remember? You went straight from tomboy to woman."

And then he kissed me. Like, really kissed me.

CHAPTER THIRTY-TWO

<u>Skyler</u>

I'm not sure about which the guys razzed me more—kissing Jonnie behind the locker rooms or crying when she'd gotten hurt? I ignored them on both fronts and stripped off my nice clothing to don my football uniform, my eyes unfocused and my thoughts somewhere far away, lying on a beach, with Jonnie next to me in that swimsuit, her hair glinting in the sunlight.

"Dude, are you even going to be able to see to throw the ball?" Logan asked.

"Maybe…" *Maybe not.*

"Derek," Logan called across the room. "We're going to need you to start on quarterback. Skyler's lovesick."

That snapped me out of my stupor. "Forget that. This is the last regular season game of my senior year.

I'm starting."

"Never mind, Derek," Logan called. "He seems to have come back to earth."

I dressed in record time, knowing the sooner I got out of the locker room, the sooner I'd see Jonnie again. Yeah, Logan was right. I was lovesick. Ugh.

Waiting outside the girls' locker room was beyond lovesick and bordered on stalking. Nine giggling cheerleaders passed me before Jonnie and Amberlyn strolled out together, arm in arm. The hottest girl on the cheerleading squad and the hottest girl on the football team.

When Amberlyn glanced up, she smiled and blushed that cheesy blush of young love. *Oh crud.* What was I supposed to do?

Just when I was trying to think of something to say, a deep voice behind me said, "Hey beautiful." Amberlyn walked right past me over to Aiden.

"Aiden?" I startled. "You can't sneak up on a guy like that, man."

"If your head wasn't so far up in the clouds, you would have noticed I've been standing beside you for approximately three minutes." Aiden glanced down at his non-existent watch.

Jonnie pulled my focus back by slipping her hand in mine. "You ready to play?"

"Huh?" I was distracted by the blue in her eyes and that hair that was still resting on her shoulders.

"Football?"

"Oh, right." I held up the ball in my other hand. "Football."

"Come on," Jonnie called as she started onto the field. "Pass me the ball."

"Go long!" I called to her. She ran, and I waited until exactly the right time, knowing instinctively when to throw based on where I knew she'd turn to catch the ball. My arm released a perfect spiral, and it flew in a high arc over thirty long yards and dropped cleanly into Jonnie's hands. Aiden and I both sighed.

"Oh my gosh," Amberlyn said with annoyance. "Guys are so weird." With that, she took off in the direction of the sidelines to meet the rest of her cheerleading squad.

"See ya after the game," Aiden called to her. She turned around and offered him a little wave. Then Aiden spoke out of the side of his mouth. "Thank you for breaking up with her."

"Mr. Morgan, that was a heck of a spiral," a voice said from behind us. We turned to see a guy in a Central Michigan University jacket and a clipboard tucked under his arm.

"Thank you, sir." I lowered my voice respectfully. Another guy stood nearby with a Ferris State jacket on. I stepped forward and shook both of their hands, and Aiden did the same.

"Mr. Becker," the guy addressed Aiden. "I understand you've improved substantially over the season."

"Thank you, sir." Aiden nodded. "I'd like to think so."

"We could use another good linebacker," the man in the Ferris State jacket said.

"Talk to me after baseball season." Aiden chuckled.

"Fair enough."

A third man stood nearby, wearing a blue jacket with a lighter-blue logo that almost looked like a Detroit Lions logo, but I realized was some sort of ocean wave. *What the heck?* He didn't approach me or Aiden but seemed distracted by our huddle of players over by the sideline.

Aiden turned around so he could whisper to only me. "Grand Rapids Tidal Waves."

"What the heck is that?" I asked softly.

"Professional," Aiden said.

"Professional what?" I was confused.

"Women's American Football League."

My head snapped toward our sideline where my beautiful girlfriend was warming up with our all-guy's team. The guy in the blue jacket was clearly watching her.

"Guess we gotta make this game count," Aiden said.

I turned back to the two men still standing beside us. "It was very nice to meet you." I shook hands with each of them, glanced again in the direction of the guy in the blue jacket ignoring me and Aiden, and chuckled.

Aiden and I jogged over to our team. He asked quietly, "Should we tell her?"

"Heck no!" I answered. "She needs to concentrate on playing this game, not showing off for a college recruiter."

"Pro," Aiden corrected me. "She's going straight to pro, dude."

CHAPTER THIRTY-THREE

Jonnie

Skyler was nervous, I could tell. I wondered if it had anything to do with the college recruiters I'd seen him talking to over by the locker rooms. "Which teams?" I asked.

"Huh?" Skyler batted his eyelashes in presumed innocence.

"Which colleges are trying to snag you?" I asked, placing my hand on my hip.

"Oh, uh, Central and Ferris," he said.

"Well, that's not too scary. They're both on your list of preferred colleges. Why do you look so nervous?"

"Nervous?" His voice cracked, and he gulped. I raised my eyebrows in question. "I'm just worried about you getting back on the field. I don't want you to get hurt again."

"Eh, I'll be fine." I swatted my hand in the air, dismissing his concern.

After a quick huddle and pep talk from our coach, the special teams' guys headed onto the field. The home team had chosen to defer to the second half, so we took the field as offense first. We didn't try any trick plays. Just clean, innocent football, taking us a few yards down the field at a time.

Skyler was avoiding giving me the ball again, but at least he was including me in the play calls. When we were twenty yards from the end zone, Skyler finally told me what I wanted to hear. The ball was coming to me.

My nerves got the better of me as I ran toward the end zone, and the ball slid right through my outstretched hands. I never got possession of it. *Darn it!*

When we got back in the huddle, Skyler ignored the rest of the guys, took my hand in his and asked point blank, "Would you be willing to try that same play again?"

"I don't know," I answered honestly.

"Do you trust me?" he asked.

"Yeah… I trust you." I gulped. *Where was he going with this?*

"I have a really specific reason why I need you to catch *this* next throw. But I can't tell you what it is until after the game." His eyes bore into mine, trying to convey some hidden message. "Just pretend we're goofing off on the beach, or that we're practicing drills, or that we're chasing after each other on the playground back in preschool."

"If you guys start making out, I'm gonna puke," Jayce said.

"Not until after the game, man." Skyler didn't even turn to look at Jayce, but a little grin pulled at the corner of his mouth and he winked at me. "I mean, I'm definitely makin' out with Jonnie after the game. You can puke if you want, I don't care."

A little giggle escaped, and I was immediately embarrassed.

"So, what's the play call?" Connor asked, sounding impatient.

"Same play?" Skyler nodded to me, wanting my confirmation.

"Just like on the beach." I returned his nod.

We broke our huddle and got into position. After the ball was snapped, I hightailed it down the field, ignoring everything around me, knowing the exact moment when to turn, knowing the ball would be at my shoulder. I snatched the ball out of the air mid-stride and finished my run into the end zone with little effort.

This was my first time holding the ball during an actual game since my accident, and it felt great. I could do this. He was right to encourage me to get back on the field. I was thankful for his confidence in me and glad he'd given me a second chance after I'd dropped the ball on the first play.

The special teams came onto the field to kick the extra point, and after that, we were on defense. Skyler, Connor, Jayce, Logan, and I brainstormed the next few plays, including Doug in the conversation since he would be a key aspect of our strategy. We wanted to keep the defense confused as much as possible, and that took effort. We planned out the whole rest of the half and managed to be tied going into half time. That was as good as could be expected playing against Rockford. They were good, but we were better. If we could stay strong through the second half.

Rockford held us off and answered us point for point throughout the entire second half. Then two minutes before the end of the game, they kicked a field goal and were up by three. The pressure was on. It took us most of that two minutes to get anywhere near the end zone. They weren't letting up the pressure.

We had ten seconds to go and were still thirty yards away with very few options. We were too far away to kick a field goal. I knew which play was our best choice, but I knew Skyler would be reluctant. Did we really want to risk using the exact play we'd used when I'd gotten hurt? Would he even dare?

During our last huddle, I took control of the conversation, not waiting for Skyler to speak, even though he was the captain.

"Guys, they have *not* been targeting me. You know it's the best play for this situation. We've practiced it a million times. I know we can do this. Let's make the last play of the last game of our senior year count. Are you with me?"

"Are you sure about this, Jonnie?" Skyler asked.

"Do you trust me?" I raised my eyebrows at him, using the same tactic he'd used at the beginning of the game.

"Yeah, babe, I trust you." He smiled that winning smile. After we broke our huddle, Skyler pulled me aside for one more little question. "We get to make out afterward, right?"

"You just get me that ball and ask me in the end zone," I told him. I sensed that little tiger growl in the back of his throat, and we hurried into position.

CHAPTER THIRTY-FOUR

<u>Skyler</u>

I couldn't believe she was brave enough to do this. I couldn't believe I'd agreed to it. As I stepped into position, everything came rushing back into my mind. The perfectly executed play, number forty-five barreling toward her, her lying on the ground, unconscious, with her arm twisted beneath her, me holding her hand while she lay on the gurney about to be whisked away in the ambulance, kissing her and telling her I loved her right there in front of a stadium full of people.

This was a bad idea.

I took a step back, risking delay of game, and several of the guys raised their heads in confusion. She never broke position but turned her head toward me and grinned.

"Trust me," she mouthed from down the line. We nodded to one another, and I got back into position. If the defense didn't know by now what play we had planned, then they never watched footage of that fateful night, and the chances of that were slim to none.

They were probably mentally calculating all the ways to stop us. I didn't care. We were doing this. We had to do this. Recruiters were watching. I had to do this for Jonnie. More than just college was on the line for her. Her career depended on this play. A career she didn't even know about yet.

I called the play. The center snapped the ball. I stepped back into the pocket, trusting Connor would protect me, trusting Logan and Jayce would hold off Rockford's cornerback long enough for Jonnie to run toward the end zone.

Just as we'd practiced thousands of times over the past thirteen years, I hauled back my arm and let the ball loose one last time. The ball sailed through the sky in a perfect arc, a perfect spiral, a perfect landing right into Jonnie's perfect hands.

I held my breath. This was out of my hands now, quite literally. This was the time when Jonnie had run into the end zone with forty-five hot on her heels. I didn't even process when the whistle blew, and the touchdown was called. All I could do was watch that cornerback barrel toward Jonnie and the whole flashback came full circle. He was going to hit her. She'd be on the ground again and this time she wouldn't be able to get back up. This had been too much of a risk. Her life was not worth a touchdown.

The cornerback barreled closer and closer as if in slow motion and passed right by her, slowing in resignation. He came to a stop and stomped his foot in frustration, then backtracked, turned around, and shook her hand in congratulations.

I ripped my helmet off as I ran toward the end zone, this time in elation rather than in panic and terror. Jonnie was safe, she'd caught the winning touchdown, and we'd won the game. I ignored all the other players and spectators. I ignored Jayce and Connor and Logan and Doug all hugging her.

When she saw me running toward her, she whipped her helmet off also, her hair falling out of its scrunchy and draping over the shoulder pads of her uniform. She'd never looked more beautiful. No polka-dotted dress, or miniskirt, or tight sweater, or swimsuit had ever improved upon this woman standing in the end zone waiting for me to swoop her up in my arms.

She wrapped her arms around my neck as I held her up and our lips met without a care about who would see us kissing in the end zone. No, making out in the end zone. Right in front of both teams, hundreds of spectators, all our parents and coaches and friends.

Oh yeah, and recruiters. Oops. I set her down, and we both laughed. She didn't even know about the guy waiting to meet her.

After we'd carried her on our shoulders and whooped and hollered and celebrated, I pulled her away from the crowd, took her by the hand, and put on a more serious expression.

"There's someone I want you to meet," I said.

She cocked her head and creased her brow. "Okay?"

I pulled her over to where I knew the man in the blue jacket from Grand Rapids Tidal Waves stood with a leather binder in his hands. I had no idea what the guy's name was, but I knew why he was here, and I knew Jonnie didn't.

"Sir," I said to the man, respectfully. "Allow me to introduce Jonnie Gillis."

"It's a pleasure to meet you, Ms. Gillis." The man held out his hand in greeting, and Jonnie rested hers in his. I took a step back and watched in pride as the girl I'd loved since preschool changed the direction of her life forever.

Oh, and I strode with confidence over to the recruiter from Central Michigan University.

EPILOGUE

<u>Jonnie</u>

"Dad, thanks again for helping me get moved into the dorms." I set down what I thought was the last of the boxes and collapsed onto the tiny bed that would be my home away from home for the next four years.

"Did Skyler get settled in last week?" Dad asked, wiping his brow.

"Yeah, they've already got the guys working out like a million hours a day, even though he won't play a single game as a freshman."

"Did I hear my name?" Skyler popped his head into my dorm room, with a grin, his hair and shirt drenched with sweat. "Hey, Mr. Gillis. Or should I call you Dr. Gillis now?" Skyler came all the way into my room and shook my father's hand.

"You'll never have him for a professor," I said, sitting up to make it easier for Skyler to lean over and kiss me. "Too much conflict of interest."

"Sorry I wasn't able to help you move in," Skyler said. "Practice ran over."

"That's okay. Coming to the college where my dad teaches means he gets to help me with things like this."

"I'm sure the free tuition was no incentive," he teased.

"Not all of us get full scholarships to play football, you know?"

"Yeah, some of us turn down opportunities to play professionally just so we can go to college," Skyler said. "After all these months, I still can't wrap my head around that."

"Eh, they didn't pay very well. Besides, I want a college education."

"That's right, young lady," my dad said in mock seriousness. "You keep your priorities in line."

"And here I thought it was because you wanted to live one building away from the hottest guy on campus," Skyler said, reaching down to help me off my bed. "I'm so excited you're finally here. I haven't seen you in weeks."

I regretted letting him pull me close. "Gross! You're sweaty and smelly. Get away from me!" I squirmed to get out of his arms.

"Come with me over to the field and throw the ball around and you can get all sweaty and smelly too." He held me firm and laughed.

"I'm still standing *right* here, guys." My dad's tone was more teasing than scolding.

"Sorry, Mr. Gillis." Skyler didn't really sound sorry. "I'll try to keep my hands off your daughter, I promise, sort of."

"I think it's time I head home." Dad scoffed at us. "Stop by for dinner occasionally, make it to all your classes Monday morning, and don't get arrested for partying this weekend."

"Athletes don't party," Skyler said. "You have nothing to worry about, Mr. Gillis."

"Says the boy who has his arms around my eighteen-year-old daughter."

"The only ulterior motive I have is to convince her to come to the football stadium so I can show her off to all my new teammates."

"You kids have fun," Dad said as he headed for the door.

"Thanks again, Daddy," I called, not really fighting Skyler's arms around me anymore. I turned my attention back to my boyfriend. "Do I really get to come with you over to the stadium?"

"Heck yeah. The guys wanna meet you," Skyler said. "Maybe they'll let you try out as a walk-on."

"Very funny. You're cute, but I don't think that would go over well."

"I wish you got to play, that's all." His face fell into a serious expression. "I know how much you love the game."

"Have you seen how large college football players

are?" I asked, grasping his arm muscles as if to prove the point. "They would flatten li'l ol' me like a pancake."

"I wouldn't let anyone hurt you." He wrapped me protectively in his arms.

"As long as we find an open field somewhere and you pass me the ball, that's all the game I need." I pulled away and looked up into his handsome face. "Because I'm your playmaker."

"You'll always be my playmaker, Jonnie." Skyler leaned in for a lingering kiss. The stadium would still be there after a few more kisses. We had four years' worth of kisses ahead of us. With a few football games and college classes thrown in here and there…

Like *Pass Me the Ball?*

Please leave a review on Julie's Author Page on Amazon and Goodreads!

Other books by Julie L. Spencer:

All's Fair in Love and Sports Series

Running to You
Meet Me at Half Court
Pass Me the Ball

Love Letters Series

Who Wants to Marry a Mormon Girl?
Who Wants to Marry a Billionaire Gamer?

Christian Women's Fiction

The Cove
The Man in the Yellow Jaguar
The Farmer's Daughter
Mending Fences: Sequel to The Farmer's Daughter
The Overlook

Buxton Peak Series

Buxton Peak: The Early Years
*Billionaire Rock Star Romance: A Buxton Peak Clean Romance (Read
in place of Book One)*
Buxton Peak Book One: Who Is Ian Taylor?
Buxton Peak Book Two: Center Stage
Buxton Peak: London Bridges
Buxton Peak Book Three: The End of the Beginning
Buxton Peak: The Complete Collection
Opening Act: Buxton Peak Meets Infusion Deep
(together with its companion story,
Opening Act: Infusion Deep Meets Buxton Peak
with co-author, Lara Wynter)

ABOUT THE AUTHOR

Julie L. Spencer raised her family in the central Michigan area where she had a very full life managing a conservation district office, writing grant proposals & book reviews, and chasing after several teenage athletes. Julie wrote her first book when she was in junior high, but prior to publishing *The Cove*, her only published work was her master's thesis. She loves to read and write New Adult Contemporary Clean fiction and has several more novels and non-fiction projects in the works.

Sign up for Julie's email newsletter at
www.subscribepage.com/JulieLSpencer-Running

Julie loves to hear from her readers and can be reached at
juliespencer1998@gmail.com

Follow Julie on Twitter @juliespencer98
www.facebook.com/JulieLSpencerAuthorPage

Check out Julie's blog at:
www.authorjuliespencer.com

52018344R00079

Made in the USA
Lexington, KY
14 September 2019